"We may be caught in unusual circumstances, but don't think for a moment my demands have changed."

Sarah's smile thinned into a tight, angry line. "You mean the big, bad reporter might churn up your son a bit emotionally, just to get some inside information?"

"I will not tolerate any infringement upon my son's privacy."

"You don't have to worry. I only eat little boys on Mondays and Wednesdays," she retorted, jabbing at his arrogance. "Today is Thursday, Your Majesty."

"Be careful, Miss Kwong," Jarek said as he advanced, crowding her, forcing her to tilt her head back to meet his eyes. In response, Sarah slapped her hand to his chest and dug her heels into the sand.

"I eat female reporters every day of the week," he warned, each syllable a low, husky rasp that sent awareness skittering up her spine.

DONNA YOUNG

CAPTIVE *of the* DESERT KING

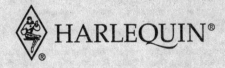

HARLEQUIN®

TORONTO • NEW YORK • LONDON
AMSTERDAM • PARIS • SYDNEY • HAMBURG
STOCKHOLM • ATHENS • TOKYO • MILAN • MADRID
PRAGUE • WARSAW • BUDAPEST • AUCKLAND

Recycling programs
for this product may
not exist in your area.

ISBN-13: 978-0-373-69415-0

CAPTIVE OF THE DESERT KING

Copyright © 2009 by Donna Young

www.eHarlequin.com

Printed in U.S.A.

ABOUT THE AUTHOR

Donna Young, an incurable romantic, lives in beautiful Northern California with her husband and two children.

Books by Donna Young

HARLEQUIN INTRIGUE
824—BODYGUARD RESCUE
908—ENGAGING BODYGUARD
967—THE BODYGUARD CONTRACT
1016—BODYGUARD CONFESSIONS
1087—SECRET AGENT, SECRET FATHER
1106—A BODYGUARD FOR CHRISTMAS
1148—CAPTIVE OF THE DESERT KING

Don't miss any of our special offers. Write to us at the following address for information on our newest releases.

Harlequin Reader Service
U.S.: 3010 Walden Ave., P.O. Box 1325, Buffalo, NY 14269
Canadian: P.O. Box 609, Fort Erie, Ont. L2A 5X3

CAST OF CHARACTERS

Sarah Kwong—A reporter who understood the meaning of "for king and country" until she uncovered dangerous palace secrets. Suddenly, she is forced to choose between a king whom she loves and a story that should be told. Is she for the king... or his country?

Jarek Al Asadi—A king who is fighting betrayal, corruption and the threat of a rebel takeover, all three well within his power to control. But when a beautiful reporter uncovers secrets that threaten her life, can he control his love for her long enough to protect her—whether she likes it or not?

Quamar Al Asadi—As advisor to his cousin, the king, Quamar has no reservations in placing his trust in diplomacy first. But when diplomacy fails to stop those threatening his family, he has no problem placing his faith in a sharp knife and a soft step, either.

Oruk Baize—A rebel leader with ambitions to seize a country his people had coveted for over two hundred years. His only obstacle? A king, a prince and an American reporter.

Murad Al Qassar—A businessman whose interest lies in export, commerce and large dividends. But when the promise of those dividends necessitate more than the usual business tactics, he has no qualms with murdering the competition—even if that competition is a royal or two.

Prince Rashid Al Asadi—A young boy destined to be king, no matter the cost. But when that cost might be his father's life, will he be able to pay?

Chapter One

They rose from the sand. Crimson vipers ready to strike.

They called themselves the Al Asheera. The Tribe.

Blood-red scarves covered their treacherous features. Machine guns filled their fists, missile launchers lay at their feet.

They were the enemies of Taer. And the time had come for the resurrection of their traitorous souls.

King Jarek Al Asadi focused his all-terrain binoculars on the army of revolutionaries clustered between the slopes of sand dunes.

They'd been bred among the brush and rock. Weaned on the grit of the earth and the blood of their enemies. Their prized possession? Not life. Nor faith. Not even family.

They valued only the land beneath their feet and the swords—honed from generations of butchery—strapped to their backs.

They believed Taer was their territory, their hunting ground.

That was their first mistake.

The Al Asheera armed the missile launchers, their movements clipped with military precision. It had been five years since they'd last surfaced. Five years since they killed Jarek's parents, kidnapped his son.

That had been their second mistake.

Fury exploded in Jarek's chest, burned the back of his throat until he nearly choked.

He shifted on his belly, burying himself deeper behind the ridge. Grimly, he scanned his enemies' horses corralled by rocks a few yards from their masters. No added supplies hung from the saddles. Only water.

Once bloated, the goatskin bags lay nearly depleted against their horses' haunches. That meant the bastards hadn't traveled far. And they weren't worried about drying out.

It also meant their prey was in the vicinity.

The palace and city lay south behind Jarek less than a half day's ride. The nearest village lay more than forty miles east. He followed the horizon just past the Al Asheera, searching for an outlining camp.

Nothing.

But he was a patient man.

The wind gusted, kicking up sand and dust. Jarek ignored the slight irritation.

He was a man born from the Sahara, carved from the wind, sand and heat—taught at a young age to endure.

The blood of kings ran hot in his veins, set the steel in his broad shoulders, the granite in his dark, chiseled features. Tradition, integrity and responsibility were his companions long before he'd understood his destiny.

Long before he understood the pain of betrayal.

Without warning, three gunshots burst from the western ridge.

Below, the signal brought the Al Asheera camp to life, their movements now more animated than precise.

The drone of an engine drifted over the wind.

Jarek followed the sound, then swore.

A four-seater plane came into view. The white, sleek bird rode low against a clear, blue sky. He didn't have to focus the binoculars to know the Royal Crest, his family's crest, was imprinted like a target on its belly.

Sarah.

Two missiles exploded from the Al Asheera encampment. On their heels came another burst of gunfire. Frustration and helplessness edged the fury, forced Jarek to draw deep, harsh breaths.

"Come on, Ramon," he whispered, silently encouraging his pilot to evade the attack.

As if hearing him, the plane banked, drawing up hard. A second later, the Al Asheera missiles rushed past its right wing, harmless.

But the maneuver cost the pilot distance. The plane faltered, then dipped over the camp, exposing its underbelly to the revolutionaries below.

A small cry of surprise exploded from behind Jarek. He swung around on his knee, his rifle leveled.

"Papa?" A boy, nearly six years in age, tugged a gray mare's reins—almost three times the boy's height—urging the animal forward.

"Rashid." Jarek swore and lowered the rifle. Trepidation raked his gut, cutting clean through to the anger, then deeper to the fear. "What are you doing here?"

A sudden burst of gunfire ripped through the stomach of the plane. A cheer rose over the wind as the engine smoked and shuddered, the aircraft struggled to maintain its altitude.

Almost instantly, the plane changed direction, heading away from the Al Asheera and toward Jarek. This time a cry of alarm rose from the camp. In mass, the revolutionaries scrambled toward their horses.

But Jarek barely noticed. The plane lost its struggle and tilted into a nosedive. His gaze followed the white blur until it crashed beyond the horizon.

"Stay, Ping." The boy dropped the reins—confident his horse would stand near his father's.

The small prince scrambled up next to Jarek.

Rashid Al Asadi stopped less than a foot from his father. Jarek noted the black eyes—intense, sharp like a well-polished, well-cut onyx.

His wife, Saree's, eyes.

The rest was Al Asadi. Beneath the soft, round face lay the promise of Jarek's square jaw and high cheekbones. And if one looked closely enough, the suggestion of a high forehead and the sharp features of Jarek's father, Makrad Al Asadi.

Jarek glanced away, unwilling to look that close.

The boy had been born with an old soul and a clever mind, Jarek's cousin, Quamar, had stated years before. A combination that equaled nothing less than an insatiable curiosity.

"Ramon?" The little boy's gaze darted past Jarek to where the plane had disappeared. Purpose was there, in the set of the boy's shoulders.

"What are you doing here, Rashid?" But his tone lost its angry edge because fear was there, too. A fear that he also saw lurking in the darkest part of his son's eyes.

"I heard you tell Uncle Quamar that you were taking a ride in the desert on Taaj before Miss Kwong arrived today," he whispered. "I thought you might want company."

Jarek had actually told Quamar that he wanted to distance himself from the American reporter, but he did not correct his son.

"You were wrong to follow me, Rashid." Jarek understood disciplining his son would have to wait, but the words would not. "And don't tell me you didn't understand that before you rode Ping out here. I imagine your tutor has Trizal searching for you as we speak. You must have worried him a great deal when you did not show up for your studies."

As Jarek's personal secretary, Trizal Lamente, had dealt with Rashid's impulsive behavior too many times in the past to react with fear but not without urgency.

Quamar, too, would be searching for them soon, if not already.

"I left Trizal a note explaining what I had done."

Jarek believed him. His son was high-spirited and head-strong, but he did not lie.

"And you think that because you told my secretary you were skipping studies, it is better?" Jarek admonished. "And your Royal Guards? Where were they?"

Before his son could answer, Jarek pulled Rashid with him to the horses. "We will discuss your disobedience later. Now we must help Ramon."

"Do you think they are dead?" Rashid's bottom lip trembled, reminding Jarek just how young his son was.

"I don't know," Jarek answered truthfully, but tempered the words with a softer tone.

Sarah's image flashed before him. The long, black hair, the vibrant green eyes, the delicate lines of her face.

Fear raked his gut. Icy and razor-sharp.

He helped his son onto Ping's back. "But if they are not, they might be injured and need our help."

The logical thing to do was to take Rashid back to the palace, then send soldiers to rescue those in the plane. But as soon as Jarek thought of it, he brushed the option aside. The soldiers would arrive too late. Even for his

son, he could not leave people to die at the hands of the
Al Asheera.

"We're going to ride fast." Jarek swung up onto Taaj.
"Can you stay with me?"

Jarek had no doubt his son could, having spent more
time riding Ping than in the classroom studying.

It was the vulnerability and the realization that his son
might have to deal with yet another death in his short life
that made Jarek wonder what else the young boy could
handle.

"Yes." The word cracked but didn't weaken the underlying resolve in Rashid's voice. "I can stay with you."

After a short, firm nod, Jarek ordered, "Let's go then."

They had very little time to reach the plane before the
Al Asheera.

With grim determination, he prodded Taaj to a full
gallop, making sure his son's horse stayed abreast.

He just prayed he wasn't risking Rashid's life in a race
toward the dead.

Chapter Two

She felt the pain, thick and hot. It rolled through her head and down to her chest—forced her to inhale deep. But with the oxygen came the stench of death, clouded with dust, tinted with blood. It caught in her throat and clogged her lungs.

She gagged, coughed, then gagged again before she pushed it all back with a shudder.

Blinking hard, Sarah Kwong focused through the blur and grit that coated her eyes. The pain was still there, jarred free with her short, jerky movements. She touched her temple, felt the wet, sticky blood against her fingers.

Slowly, she lifted her head and took in the damage surrounding her.

The nose and cockpit were no more than gnarled steel buried deep under sand. The pilot, Ramon, lay slumped against the instruments of the plane. The windshield had shattered on impact. Shards of glass covered the pilot's head and upper body.

"Ramon?"

Blood matted his gray hair and coated his forehead and face in a wide, crimson mask.

She hit the release button on her seat belt and slid to the

space between their seats. Vertigo hit her in waves. She stopped, caught her breath, calmed the nausea.

At sixty, Ramon had three decades on her. But with a forthcoming smile and easy banter, the pilot formed an instant rapport with her on their flight from Morocco.

She scooted forward and placed her fingers against his neck.

His pulse was weak and fluttery. Still, he had one.

Carefully, she pulled him back into his seat. Blood soaked his polo shirt, turning the navy blue a crimson black. A shard of glass, the size of her forearm, protruded from his chest. Sarah's gut tightened in protest over the bits of bone and jagged skin that clung to its toothed edges.

The sun beat down on the plane, thickening the air to a rancid oven heat. Sweat stung her eyes. Impatiently she wiped it away, then glanced around for something to stem the flow of his blood.

Fear tightened her chest, forcing her to exhale in a long, shaky breath. "Don't you dare die on me, Ramon," she threatened, hoping her words would jar the injured man awake.

She'd dressed in cream-colored cotton pants, a matching long-sleeved blouse and—aware of convention in a foreign country—a camisole beneath for modesty sake.

Quickly, she unbuttoned her blouse, slipped it off, then ripped the material down the back and into two pieces.

She placed the first half under his head and pressed the second against the flow of blood from his chest.

"Don't touch it." The command was weak and raspy with pain.

But her relief came swift, making her voice tremble enough to draw the pilot's gaze. "Don't talk," she warned, while her fingers probed lightly, judging the depth of his chest wound. "Save your strength."

Ramon struggled to keep his leather-brown eyes on her. Blood ran from his mouth, dripped from his chin. "It doesn't matter now."

"Don't talk like that," she snapped, the harshness more from fear than irritation or anger. "I just need to stop the bleeding—"

"It's too late." The words struggled past the moist rattle that filled his chest.

Ramon's hand slid to his side. He pulled his gun from its holster. "Take this. Protect yourself," he gasped. He shoved it at her until she took the pistol. "Grab the survival kit. Run."

"Run from who?"

"Roldo." He grasped at her arm. Blood made his fingers slick, while the loss of blood made his grip weak. "Go now."

"I can't leave—"

"Tell the king I'm sorry."

Before Sarah could answer him, Ramon's hand fell to the floor, limp.

Sarah had seen death before. Many times. But always behind yellow crime scene tape with a microphone in her hand and a camera over her shoulder.

Her fingers fluttered over his cheek, then closed his eyes.

Never had death brushed this close, or been this personal. The finality left her cold and empty.

Sarah swore and pressed her fingers into her eyes, averting the prick of tears, easing the throb of pain.

Suddenly, a horse whinnied to the right of the plane.

Sarah grabbed the gun and thumbed the safety off.

"Ramon."

She aimed the pistol at the door. "Come through that door and it will be the last thing you do," Sarah yelled.

"Don't shoot, damn it. It's Jarek, Sarah." The sharp voice came from the outside—a command not a question. Only one man had a voice like that—the deep, haunting timbre, the edges clipped with a hint of a British accent.

When the passenger door slammed open, she was already lowering the pistol. "Your Majesty, this is a surprise."

Coal-black eyes swept over her, taking in her slender frame, the pale skin.

She knew what he was thinking. Delicate. Reserved. Harmless. That's what most people thought.

What he'd thought all those years ago. Before he got to know her.

"Are you injured?" He nodded toward the blood-soaked camisole.

"No." She lied without qualm, her eyes studying the man. He hadn't changed much over the past eight years. Leaner, more rigid, maybe. He dressed casually in tan riding breeches, a white linen shirt and black riding boots. The clothes were tailored and fit snugly over his broad shoulders, lean hips and long, masculine legs.

He certainly had the look of a desert king: an indigo scarf wrapped around his head, his sharp angled features, his skin bronzed from the sun and slightly grooved from the elements.

His eyes narrowed as they met hers.

Something shifted inside her. Fear? Relief? "Ramon is dead."

Jarek glanced over at the pilot, but the king's features remained stiff, emotionless. Only the slight tightening of his jaw gave away the fury beneath the indifference. Sarah realized she would have missed it if she hadn't been studying his features so intently.

Then quickly, before she could react, he caught her chin, turned her head and examined her wound. "Any dizziness? Nausea?"

"No," she lied again, resisting the urge to touch her temple. Telling Jarek about her headache wouldn't change the situation.

She looked beyond his shoulder and through the door to the empty desert. "Any others coming?"

"No." He released her. "Just myself. And Rashid."

"Rashid?" Sarah repeated, surprised. "The prince is here?"

"Yes." His mouth flattened to a hard, almost bitter line. A mouth, she remembered, that heated with passion or curved wickedly with humor.

"We have very little time. I didn't see any jeeps with the Al Asheera. Only horses. But that doesn't mean they don't have them," Jarek added. He took Ramon's gun from her grip, then pulled her from between the seats.

"Behind you is the survival kit. Water, rations, first aid. On the floor…" he pointed under the seats "…flares."

"Got it," she answered, but the first thing she snagged was her purse—a brown, leather hobo bag that had seen better days.

"Forget your purse. Take what's important. Water first."

"My purse is important. It won't get in the way." Quickly, she slipped it over her neck and one shoulder. She grabbed the survival kit and the extra sack of water. It took her a moment to find the flares hidden under a broken passenger seat in the back. She shoved several into her purse, along with a loose flashlight and gloves.

Jarek leaned over and checked the pilot's pulse. After a moment, he cupped the older man's cheek. "May Allah keep you always, my friend."

Sarah turned away, uncomfortable with her intrusion.

She stumbled from the plane, nearly landing face-first in the scrub and sand.

"Great," she muttered. Impatient, she reached down and broke the heels off her shoes, trying not to think about how much the cost of the tan slingbacks had set back her budget a few months earlier.

"Miss Kwong?"

All boy. That was Sarah's first thought as she looked at Rashid. His eyes were big and wide and black as midnight. Almost too big for the small body, the baby-soft features.

"Your Highness."

He dressed like his father in the riding pants and boots. His scarf, just a tad off center, revealed sooty black hair spiking in sweaty strands against his cheeks and ears.

"I am glad to see you are unharmed," the little boy greeted her in a quiet voice. Those big eyes looked past her shoulder to the plane even as he helped her with the supplies.

"Is Ramon safe?"

Sarah knelt down in front of him and laid her hand on his shoulder. "I'm sorry, Your Highness," Sarah explained, gently. "Ramon did not survive."

"I see," he whispered. His throat worked spasmodically against tears. "My father?"

"He's saying goodbye."

Jarek stepped out to the sand. In one hand, he carried a scarf—Ramon's head scarf—filled with more supplies. In the other hand, he carried Ramon's pistol. "Rashid—"

"I know, Papa. Miss Kwong explained." The words were quiet, but resolute. Sarah saw the tears swell in the young prince's eyes and how he bit his lip to keep them from falling.

Sarah stood, but left her hand on the boy's shoulder long enough for a gentle squeeze of encouragement.

"There is nothing we can do for Ramon," Jarek added, his gaze narrowing over her gesture. "Please let go of my son, Miss Kwong."

The emotions punched hard, an angry swipe at her solar plexus. Resentment. Humiliation. Rage. She fought them all as she dropped her hand.

Eight years of denial fell away, lying like broken chains at her feet.

She'd come three thousand miles to see. To finally know. And now she did.

Nothing had changed.

"Miss Kwong, have you ridden?" Jarek asked briskly, his gaze now on the horizon.

"Yes. But it's been a long time." Too long, she added silently and resisted the urge to rub her temples where the pain was centered.

"You'll ride Ping." He nodded toward the gray mare. "Give me the backpack. You can keep your purse."

He tied the scarf and supplies to Ping's saddle. "Rashid, come hold the horse steady."

"It's okay, girl." The little boy held the bridle and stroked the horse's nose.

"Grab the pommel," Jarek ordered Sarah, then glanced down at her foot. Noticing the broken heels, he raised an eyebrow in question.

"They're styled to make a great impression, not for an afternoon hike in the sand."

"I assure you. You've always made an impression. Without the shoes," he murmured, then motioned her to lift her foot.

She placed her heel in his palm, felt the slight dusting of his thumb against her ankle. Her toes curled, but her back stiffened.

"Don't," she snapped, low and mean.

"Don't what?"

"Don't tell me not to touch your son one minute, then stroke me the next."

"Rashid and Ramon were very close," Jarek replied, his answer matching the hushed tone of hers. "If you had comforted him for much longer, the tears would've taken over and made things more difficult. My priority is his protection. We will have time for grief, but only after we are safe." Then, almost deliberately, his thumb grazed her ankle again. "Now. Are you ready?"

Before she could reply, he boosted her into the saddle.

Ping bristled against the weight, stomping her front foot for a moment before a few murmured words from Rashid settled her down.

Quickly, Sarah adjusted her purse across her back and out of her way.

"Here you are, Miss Kwong." Rashid handed her the reins.

When the boy turned away, Ping took a step forward, causing Sarah to lock her thighs on the saddle. "Whoa, girl."

"Are you going to be all right?" Rashid asked, his small brow knitted with concern.

"I'll be fine, Your Highness. It's like falling off a horse, right?" Sarah winked.

The little boy smiled. A big smile that revealed a dimple in each cheek.

A small rubber band of emotion snapped inside her chest. She knew in that moment, if she wasn't careful, she'd be a sucker for those dimples.

"Ping will follow Taaj, Miss Kwong. So all you have to do is stay in that saddle," Jarek ordered. "If you hear gunshots, don't look back. Do you hear me?"

"Yes."

"And keep up." Jarek lifted Rashid onto Taaj, then swung up into the saddle behind him.

"Papa, look," Rashid shouted.

A long line of dust clouds rose over the horizon behind them.

Sarah raised her hand to shield the sun. "What is it? A sandstorm?"

She'd read about the dangers of the desert—scorpions, vipers, raging winds of sand, but didn't think she would ever experience any firsthand.

Jarek swore and reached for his binoculars.

"The Al Asheera. The same who gunned down the airplane. They've spread out and are approaching at a full gallop."

Suddenly the sand exploded no more than fifty feet in front of them.

Ping reared back and spun herself away. Sarah grabbed the pummel and held her seat. "Whoa!"

"Rockets," Jarek warned and pointed to the west. "Head toward those cliffs. We can hide in the caves."

"Away from the city?" Sarah exclaimed, her head still ringing from the explosion.

"They've blocked our route back to the palace. Go!"

Another blast hit fifty feet to their side, narrowly missed the king and his son.

In an instant, both horses raced across the dunes. Sarah leaned close to Ping's neck. The horse was breathing hard but Sarah didn't dare slow her down.

"They're deliberately driving us farther into the desert," Jarek shouted.

Gunshots burst through the air, causing little explosions that nipped at the heels of their horses.

The Al Asheera's cries shot across the sand. Their red

robes brazen in the sunlight, the rifles raised against their shoulders.

"They're gaining on us, Ping," Sarah warned the horse, then gripped the saddle tighter to keep her seat.

Suddenly, Jarek pointed toward an outcropping of jagged, black stones jutting up from the sand. "Head for the rocks!"

"Come on, girl!" Sarah urged. The horse raced through the dunes and scrub to the field of rock.

Jarek pulled Taaj to a halt at the edge and checked the wind. "It's blowing in the right direction. Let's hope it stays that way."

Sarah offered a brief prayer of thanks when Ping stopped alongside Taaj. "They're coming, Jarek." Without realizing it, Sarah said his name. He stiffened beside her, but otherwise didn't say anything.

He slid off Taaj and gave the reins to Rashid. "Get as far into the field as you can, then wait for me. Go slow enough so the horses can find footing. The last thing we need is for them to break a leg."

Bullets strafed the rocks a few yards behind him.

"Did you grab the flares from the cockpit?" Jarek asked.

"Yes."

"How many?"

"Four."

"Give them to me."

She dug into her purse until her fingers touched plastic caps. "Here."

He tucked the end of the scarf over his face, then snapped the lids off two flares and struck the ends against a nearby rock. "Go!"

Sarah followed Rashid over the broken bits of stone. "What is he doing?"

Sparks shot from the flares. Jarek tossed one, then another toward the edge of the rock bed.

"Look." Rashid pointed to the edge of shale.

Almost instantly, a fire fluttered over the ground in an orange haze of heat.

"That's not big enough—"

"Watch," Rashid responded, cutting her off.

Within moments, smoke rose from the flames, dense with sulphur, black with oil, until it stood twenty feet high—and more than thirty times that in length.

"The smoke is too thick for them to see the ground," Rashid explained, but the young boy's eyes never left his father.

"They can't bring their horses in over the rocks without risking injury."

"They could walk them through," Sarah answered, her eyes never wavering from Jarek.

"It would take too long. They would pass out from the fumes."

The dark cloud gathered strength, rolling over the rocks as it grew in girth. Jarek scraped the last two flares against the stone, turned and was swallowed whole.

Sarah held her breath. The fumes stung her nostrils, coated her lungs.

In the distance they could hear horses scream. Men yelled obscenities. Gunshots bounced behind them, too far to cause damage.

Jarek. Sarah's mind screamed his name, willing him to reappear.

Suddenly, he broke from the darkness, running after the horses.

Within moments, he swung up behind his son. His scarf was gone from his face. Black streaks smudged his cheek, across his forehead. But otherwise he appeared no worse for the experience.

"That was close." She exhaled slowly, hoping to settle the pounding in her head, the queasiness that slapped at the back of her throat. He was safe. They were safe.

"You think we're safe?"

Startled, she realized she'd spoken the words out loud.

"Yes." She glanced back. The river of fire and smoke had widened the distance between them and the Al Asheera. "Safer than we were a few moments ago."

Jarek's gaze flickered over her. "Do you know how to pray, Miss Kwong?"

"Yes." Hadn't she just done that very thing for him?

"Then I suggest you start," Jarek answered grimly. "Because this only delayed them. Next time, they'll be more prepared."

Chapter Three

"Are you going to tell me what this is all about?"

Jarek glanced at the woman beside him, fought the irritation that she provoked just with her presence.

"Oil shale." It wasn't the answer she was looking for, but the only one he was willing to give at this point.

His gaze swept over her face, in spite of himself. It had been awhile since he'd seen her. A lifetime since he tasted her, felt her give beneath him.

Since then, Sarah Kwong had become a household name—less here than in America—but recognizable nonetheless. At thirty, she was the most recent rising star in the news correspondence business.

Unaware of the adult tension, the little boy grew excited over the topic. "I've never seen the shale burn like that before, right, Papa?"

Jarek gave Rashid a reassuring squeeze but didn't answer him. He wasn't about to have any kind of personal conversation with his son while a reporter looked on.

"But you've seen it burn before?" Sarah asked, with a hint of a smile.

Her lips were full, her mouth just short of wide, but with enough curve to leave one wondering if she understood some hidden secret. A secret that reached the feminine arch of her brows, the deep green of her irises.

Heat curled deep in his gut, stroked the base of his spine.

Jarek recognized the sensation for what it was, cursed it for what it meant.

"Many times—"

"Here in the desert, you can't always find brush or wood for a fire, so people use the shale for heat and cooking," Jarek interrupted his son.

Undeterred, Rashid continued, "They also use camel dung. I've seen Grandpa Bari's people use it."

"Do you mean Sheik Bari Al Asadi?"

"Yes," his son replied. "He isn't my real grandpa, but I call him that, anyway. My real grandpa died before I was born."

"Do you visit him often—"

"Is this an interview, Miss Kwong?" Jarek interrupted.

"No," she answered slowly, her tone cold enough to blast the heat from his words. "It's a conversation with a little boy."

"I didn't realize with reporters there was a difference," Jarek responded, his words sharp with warning. Rashid tensed against him, but in confusion, not fear, Jarek was sure.

"There is, Your Majesty. Maybe when we have time, I can explain the difference," she answered, impressing him with how she controlled the edge of sarcasm in her voice.

"I look forward to it." Jarek deliberately took the sting from his words for Rashid's sake. Still, he took some male satisfaction in the momentary confusion that flashed across Sarah's features and the sudden awareness that widened her eyes.

"Once the palace realizes your plane went down and that I'm missing, they'll send out a search party."

"How long will that take?"

Absently, she brushed a thick lock of black hair back over a bare shoulder. Pink flushed the tips of her shoulders, spotted the soft curve of her cheeks.

Around her neck, she wore a simple jade pendant, the same deep green of her eyes. Its shape oval, the chain, a fine gold rope. A gift, she'd told him once, from her grandmother. A kindred spirit.

The white camisole did little to protect her from the elements and only emphasized the slender bones, the delicate, almost fragile, frame.

But it was the blood, a long streak that had crusted from her temple to her earlobe, that had sniped at him since they'd left the plane.

Jarek bit back a curse. Delicate or not, she had hung on, with a fierce determination that hiked her chin, set her spine ramrod straight. No tears. No hysteria. Plenty of courage.

He pulled a long, white scarf from his saddle bag and handed it to her. "Put this over your head. The scarf will keep you from burning."

She put the scarf over the top of her head, crisscrossed it at the front of her throat before placing the ends back over her shoulders.

Years of need and longing tightened inside him, threatening to snap his control. He remembered the way she'd softened in his arms. Warm. Pliable. The brazen boldness that always gave way in a shudder of sweet surrender.

"Did Ramon radio a distress call?" Jarek asked, more to divert his thoughts, since he already suspected her answer.

"No. We had no time."

"Then the rescue will not happen before tomorrow. We'll need to find shelter for tonight."

THE SAHARA WAS DRY AND SPITEFUL. The wind slapped at them, its edges sharp with grit and heat.

"We'll stop here and rest the horses," Jarek ordered, and dismounted Taaj with Rashid.

Sarah grimaced and swung down from Ping, her movements jerky and stiff. They'd left the shale field hours earlier, heading farther west through scrub and rock.

"If you are sore, stretch out your legs or they'll cramp," Jarek suggested, his tone rigid.

"I'll just do that," Sarah answered, noting that Jarek had already walked away.

He was tall with the arrogant stance of a warrior, and with it, the confidence that comes with royal blood.

"I thought camels were the preferred mode of transportation here," Sarah murmured. The man walked in long, steady strides. His breeding set every muscle, every bone, every motion.

The wind whipped the end of her scarf against her face. Giving into impulse, she rubbed the soft cotton against her cheek and inhaled the scents of spice and saddle leather.

"Camel riding would make you no less sore," Rashid whispered as he maneuvered under Ping's neck. "You're just out of shape."

Sarah smiled at the boy's candor. "All that money I spent at the gym has gone to waste."

"You should buy a horse like Ping." Rashid stroked the mare's nose.

"No, thank you, sport. I'll keep my membership at the gym, even if it isn't helping."

Rashid grinned, dimples flashing. "My Aunt Anna calls me 'sport,' also."

"I'm sorry, Your Highness, I didn't mean—"

"That's all right. You have my permission to do so in private. I like the name. It's very American." He glanced around Ping's neck and spotted Jarek watering Taaj. "Just don't use the name around my father. It will be our secret."

"Our secret," Sarah agreed, unable to resist the young boy's charm. She just wondered how much that secret was going to cost her in the future.

No more than she'd paid in the past, she mused and wondered if they guillotined their enemies in Taer.

Sarah hated small planes, hated job restrictions more, but she would have flown the whole three thousand miles in a cardboard box—with dozens of hoops to jump through—for a chance at this interview. A chance to see Jarek and put the past to rest.

There were rules attached, of course. No cell phone. No cameras. No personal questions about his son, or his late wife or any other family member for that matter.

In consideration of his requests she hadn't brought much with her. Jarek had allowed nothing more than a miniature recorder for interview notes. Which meant only questions about Taer, now that Taer had agreed to deal with the United States over the small country's crude oil supply.

The picture restriction, she could handle. Even the cell phone restriction.

The personal questions were going to be tough.

No fuss, no obstacles. In and out before their Annual Independence Ball, Jarek had insisted.

Or no admittance.

"Sarah, what happened to your purse?"

Sarah followed Rashid's finger to a hole in the side of her bag.

"I don't know." Quickly, she unzipped the purse and dug through its contents.

"It's a bullet," Rashid exclaimed. "Your purse stopped a bullet."

Her fingers touched her wallet. A brand-new vintage, slim envelope wallet that she'd bought for the trip. But when she pulled it out, the leather nearly fell apart in her hand. Tucked between shattered credit cards and a ripped checkbook, was the slug.

"I guess it did," she agreed, then dug through the rest of her things until she found her digital voice recorder. One side showed a small dent but no other marks. She pressed the record button.

"Does it work still?"

"Let's see." Sarah pressed the playback button. *Does it work still?*

A smile tugged at the prince's lips. "You are very fortunate. If you hadn't had your purse, you'd have been shot in the back."

"I'd have to agree, Your Highness." Sarah fished through the rest of her things and after a few minutes decided only her wallet had suffered any real damage. She tried not to think about how close that bullet had come to severing her spine.

As if reading her mind, Ping snorted and shook her head.

Sarah laughed, very much aware her reaction was more nerves than humor. "You can say that again."

"She does that for attention," Rashid admitted. "My father says she is vain. But she is allowed to be since she is a beautiful horse."

"She is very beautiful," Sarah agreed. "May I pet her?"

Rashid considered the request for a long moment. "Yes. But know that sometimes she bites the grooms when they handle her."

Sarah ran her fingers over Ping's nose, making sure the horse would catch the scent of Jarek's scarf.

"She likes you," Rashid commented, obviously impressed. "She doesn't like anyone except me. And my father, of course."

"I think she only likes me because you are standing here," Sarah assured him. "But I'm glad she didn't bite me."

Feeling her muscles tighten, Sarah stepped back and bent over sideways to stretch out the stiffness. "Do you ride often, Your Highness?"

"Everyday, if I can. Taaj and Ping are Arabian horses. So they are conditioned for the desert," Rashid replied, watching Sarah with an idle curiosity. "They enjoy it, too."

"Do you and your father ride often together?"

"No," Rashid admitted slowly. "He is far too busy. So I try not to bother him."

Rashid's statement came out with a practiced, almost robotic ease.

"Is that what your father told you?"

"No. Not really." Rashid pretended to straighten Ping's bridle and didn't say any more.

Sarah decided to change the subject. "You know, I used to ride a long time ago." She shifted, then stretched to the opposite side.

"You haven't forgotten," Rashid commented with six-year-old diplomacy. "You held your seat well enough."

"Gee, thanks," Sarah murmured, then straightened.

Rashid laughed. "You did look funny bouncing around, though, Sarah." He froze, embarrassed. "I'm sorry. I didn't mean to be rude."

"That's all right. I'm sure it was funny. And I prefer to be called Sarah," she replied, winking. "Our secret?"

"Yes." Rashid tried to wink, but succeeded only in making both eyes flutter.

Jarek approached, effectively cutting off Sarah's laughter.

"Rashid, water Ping over by Taaj, please." His words were even and contained no censure, surprising Sarah. He handed his son a feed bag filled with water. "Make sure you drink some water, too, Rashid."

"Yes, Papa." Rashid paused, noting the rifle Jarek held in his other hand. "You think the Al Asheera are close?"

"No. But I want to be sure," Jarek replied, solemnly. "I'm going to the nearest ridge. I want to check our tracks and get my bearings. We cannot risk mistakes."

Jarek waited until Rashid led his horse away, before he turned to Sarah. "I realize we are caught in unusual circumstances. But don't think for a moment my demands have changed."

Sarah's smile thinned into a tight, angry line. "You mean the big, bad reporter might churn up your son a bit emotionally, just to get some inside information?"

"Exactly. I will not tolerate any infringement upon my son's privacy," Jarek remarked.

"You don't have to worry. I only eat little boys on Mondays and Wednesdays," she retorted, jabbing at his arrogance. "Today is Thursday, Your Majesty."

"Be careful, *Miss Kwong*." Jarek advanced, crowding her, forcing her head back to meet his eyes. Sarah slapped her hand to his chest, dug her heels into the sand.

The black eyes flickered over her hand, then back to her face, telling her what he thought of her stand against him.

"I eat female reporters every day of the week," he warned, each syllable a low, husky rasp that sent awareness skittering up her spine.

Pride stopped her fingers from curling into his shirt. But

it was the flash of desire in the deepest part of Jarek's gaze that made them tremble.

Jarek swung away, leaving her to watch him in stunned silence. She crossed her arms over her chest, knowing the self-protective move wouldn't have helped her one bit if he'd followed through on his threat.

"You shouldn't make him angry," Rashid admonished, coming to stand at her side. "It won't help our situation."

Sarah raised an eyebrow. "How old are you?"

"Six."

"Sure you're not thirty?" she commented wryly and watched Jarek crest the dune. If anyone was comfortable in their skin, it was Jarek Al Asadi. His muscles were well-defined and fluid, his stride purposeful.

"My Uncle Quamar said I have an old soul with new bones," Rashid said, shrugging. "Whatever that means."

"It means you are smart for your age." Sarah pulled him to her side for a quick, reassuring hug.

"Sarah, can I tell you something?" Rashid's tone turned serious.

"Sure, sport."

"Papa didn't know I had followed him from the palace into the desert this morning," Rashid confessed. "I snuck past my guards and the horse handlers."

"You snuck past…into the desert…" Sarah stopped and closed her eyes for a moment. All the scenarios of what could have happened to the child raced through Sarah's mind.

"Sweet Lord," she whispered.

"He didn't find out until after you and Ramon crashed." Rashid stepped away from her, his little body stiff, his face set. "So if my father seems angry, it's because of me. I'm sorry."

THE ANGER RODE HIGH on Jarek's shoulders, put the rigidness in his long, quick strides. But it was desire that constricted his gut, left him aroused.

And made him run, damn it. For the second time in one day.

Jarek stopped just short of the ridge top. Anything higher would make him a target.

The Al Asheera were out there. Not far behind them, he was sure.

Scowling, Jarek narrowed his eyes against the sun's glare, peered through the rippling heat waves that floated above the desert floor and shimmered against the sandstone cliffs just beyond.

The wind had died hours before. Sweat trickled from his temples, down his cheeks, itched the scarred skin of his back.

He sat back on his haunches, snatched off his head scarf and hit it against his thigh.

Laughter drifted toward him. Hers. His son's. Both light, both a little hesitant—as with any budding friendship.

Jarek grit his teeth. The last thing he wanted was his son to befriend an ex-lover. Especially a woman reporter with heavy-lidded cat eyes and a smart mouth.

Forcing his frustration back, Jarek studied the terrain. The Sahara was little more than a vast, empty void of beige, spotted here and there with tufts of brittle brush, cracked earth and broken rock.

He searched for movement—a stirring of dust, a glint of steel, branches that had no business moving in the thick, oppressive air.

At one time Jarek had been military. A necessary

vocation for the royal. A man could not lead, unless he also served, his father always said.

Training and instincts told him there would be trackers sent through the smoke. Men who understood the barest scratch against stone, the slightest swirl of sand that was once a footprint.

He slid his rifle across his thighs, let the weight of it remind him he had killed before and would likely kill again before they reached safety.

With a hiss of displeasure, a lizard scurried from its shaded cover beneath a nearby saltbush.

Jarek hit the sand sideways, his rifle ready, his finger tight on the trigger. A flash of red cloth—no more than a millisecond of warning—and Jarek fired.

The rifle exploded, on its heels came a cry of pain, the thud of a body against the ground.

He crawled on elbows and knees, ignoring the burn of the sand beneath him. Within moments, he reached the Al Asheera soldier.

Jarek's nostrils flared at the scent of blood and soured sweat. The rifle bullet struck the rebel's face, leaving torn skin and shattered bone in its place. Quickly, Jarek searched his pockets but found only a few dollars and a small bag of hashish.

A buzzard circled above, his screeches marked his territory for those who needed warning.

"Don't worry," Jarek muttered, but already his gaze scanned the immediate perimeter. The Al Asheera always traveled in pairs.

"Where's your partner?" Jarek asked the dead man. "Running for help?"

Jarek blinked the sweat from his eyes, allowing a moment for the sting to fade. If he tracked the soldier, he'd leave Rashid and Sarah vulnerable. And that was unacceptable.

Instead, he scrambled down the slope, cursing fate with each step.

It was time to run. Again.

Chapter Four

The man woke. Tense. Alert. Ready for an attack.

He laid quietly for a moment, listening for the rustle of the tent, the footsteps on the ground outside. A habit he'd developed from childhood. A habit that had saved his life more than once over the years.

"Master Baize. Your guest is here." The voice pierced through the curtain, its tone deep and heavily accented.

Oruk Baize forced his muscles to relax. "Give me a minute, Roldo, then send him in."

A quiet sigh caught Oruk's attention. Slowly, he slid the silk sheet from the warm body beside him. The material hissed over a supple white shoulder, down the slender curves and smooth back to round, naked buttocks.

For a moment, he thought about opening the window flap, allowing the sunlight to pierce the darkness—maybe burn off the stale scent of sex and sweat that still hung heavy in the air. It'd be worth the tongue lashing he'd receive, to see her pale skin heat in temper.

Besides, he might be up for a good fight, he mused, silently. Something he'd grown accustom to over the months, and now actually anticipated.

He threw the sheets back over the woman and stepped

from the bed. Seduction, domination. A little of both. The thought made him hard, then annoyed.

Business before pleasure.

Oruk pulled on a pair of dark, silk trousers and zipped them enough to cover his hips. No need to exert too much energy.

After all, this associate would be dead soon.

He stepped through the curtain opening and into the main part of the tent.

Oruk was a big man, with wide shoulders and a deep, barreled chest. His features were that of a soldier—broad, flat and unyielding. But attractive enough to have his bed warmed most nights.

He was the son of a camp follower. Most were, in the Al Asheera. He'd never known his father and barely re-membered his mother—a whore who had deserted him when he was nine.

He'd survived like most of his kind. At ten, he'd learned to shoot a gun, throw a knife. By eleven, he'd killed with them.

Oruk walked to the opposite side of the tent and stopped by his teakwood coffee table. Some comforts he refused to give up, even when he was forced to act as a nomad.

That included good whiskey. And even better, a smoke.

He opened a nearby humidor and selected a cigar. Cuban. Expensive. And the only brand he smoked.

The tent rustled. He felt a short gust of wind, heard the hard step of man in a hurry. "Hello, Murad." He clipped off the end of the cigar and lit it with a match.

"We had a deal, Baize."

Oruk ignored the slight tone of contempt in the other man's voice. "Aren't you supposed to be at the office?"

He took several deep puffs, but didn't offer the businessman a cigar. *Why waste a good cigar?* Oruk thought with derision.

"They escaped from the plane wreckage."

Murad Al Qassar was a businessman by trade, an accountant by looks. With short trimmed hair and long, thin features, he was the only man Oruk knew who wore a pin-striped suit and a tie to an Al Asheera camp.

"I know," Oruk finally answered. "Roldo told me."

Roldo Costo threw himself onto the pile of pillows in the corner of the tent and shrugged. "Things happen."

Roldo was a little man with greasy hair and rotted teeth. Still, Oruk did not keep him employed for his looks, only for his talents.

"The king decided at the last minute not to meet the reporter in Morocco. There is little we can do about that," Oruk pointed out.

"I disagree," Murad snapped.

"The king won't get away from my men again, Murad." Roldo took out his knife and began cleaning his finger-nails, a habit Oruk knew Murad found disgusting. It was the exact reason why Roldo did it whenever the business-man came around.

"Luckily for us, he was there in the desert," Roldo added. "He watched Ramon's plane go down. We're tracking them to the caves."

"Who?" Murad demanded. "Ramon and Jarek?"

"The reporter, the king and his son," Oruk inserted. "So you see, Murad, things are working out in our favor."

"The prince?" Murad took a moment to digest that bit of information. "What about Ramon?"

"He's dead," Oruk explained. "Roldo found him in the cockpit. Or what was left of him."

"That's not good enough, Oruk." Murad eyes narrowed. "We had a deal. One that's cost me a tremendous amount of money."

Oruk studied the red tip of his cigar. "There is nothing to worry about. Instead of being on the plane, the king was in the desert with his son. An outing of sorts. Fate placed him and the boy in the vicinity of the crash site."

"I don't believe in fate."

"Destiny, then." Oruk smiled at his own joke. "Either way, it is good luck for us."

Murad swore. "And yet the king is still alive."

"Like I said." Roldo shoved his knife back in his boot and stood. "My men have staked out the caves and are waiting to move in at daylight. The cliffs are too risky in the dark. I'll lose good men."

"Take the risk," Murad snapped, his lips curling back on his teeth in anger. He stepped up to Roldo, going toe-to-toe with the mercenary. "We had an agreement. The king and his son dead. They've accommodated you by being together, don't mess it up. We haven't been able to get this close to him or his son in a long time. Understand me?"

"I understand that you will take care of the buyers and the shipments," Oruk answered for Roldo. He walked to the bar cart to pour himself a shot of whiskey. "And I will take care of the Royals and your gambling debts once we have control of Taer."

"I also provided the weapons," Murad reminded him.

"And I provided the Al Asheera," Oruk countered, then signaled Roldo to step away from Murad. When the little man moved, Oruk continued. "We are all doing our part."

"I'll believe that, Oruk, when Roldo takes care of the king and his son."

"In my time, Murad." Oruk's tone hardened. "Not yours."

"Time is running out," Murad warned. "Soon Jarek will sign the agreement with the Americans."

"Agreed." Oruk flicked his ashes, let them fall to the rug. "But once we control the throne, it will not matter. The death of the reporter will only widen the rift with the Americans."

"What about his cousin, Quamar? And Sheik Bari?"

"I imagine Quamar will be searching soon," Oruk reasoned. "It will take time for him to notify Bari. By then, we'll have the king and his son."

"You had better." Murad pulled back the tent opening. "I have a meeting in the city. Notify me when you have them."

Roldo spat on the ground after Murad left. "He whines too much."

"And you screwed up." Irritation scraped at Oruk's nerves, but he forced the emotion back. Understanding the mentality of the mercenary, made it easier to control him. "Bring me the Royals and you will have the pleasure of killing Murad when its time."

"I would like that."

The bed curtain flickered and Oruk's loins grew heavy. He finished the shot of whiskey, then put down his glass.

"Screw up again, Roldo, and I will punish you myself." Oruk held one side of the curtain open and stepped partway through before turning back to the little man. "Do you understand me?"

"Yes. I understand." Roldo waited until Oruk disappeared, then he spit again.

This time in front of the curtain.

"WE'LL REST FOR A MOMENT and let the horses breathe a little," Jarek ordered, then pulled on Taaj's reins. He leaned down and whispered in his son's ear, then pointed to a small niche in the wall a few feet away.

"It cannot be too much farther, Sarah," Rashid told her as he slid off his father's horse. "Once the path widens, I'm sure we'll find shelter."

Jared had stopped mid-height of the sandstone cliffs—a monument of jagged stone and sheered walls, all striped in burnt hues of rust and beige and black shadows.

The evening wind skittered across the dunes, now washed in golden hues from the fading sun.

"It really is beautiful, isn't it?" Sarah murmured.

"Uncle Quamar says that for those who learn to respect the Sahara, her true beauty is revealed," Rashid explained.

The little boy had dozed for most of the two-hour trip, leaving nothing but a tension-filled silence between Sarah and his father.

"Your Uncle Quamar seems to say quite a bit, doesn't he?" Sarah slid from her saddle, happy to give her backside the respite.

"He certainly does," Jarek commented wryly, then jabbed a thumb at the long wall of cliffs. "There are caves in between the rocks and crevices. We've only a little farther to go before we find shelter in one of them. But from here on, we'll need to travel on foot," Jarek instructed.

"I'm beginning to think, I'm more of the 'wave down a taxi with air conditioning' type of person, Your Highness. No offense to your horse, Prince Rashid."

"I'm sure she isn't insulted." Rashid patted Ping's neck, just to be sure then nodded toward the niche. "I have to…" He paused, then grinned. "Take care of business."

"Oh, you do, do ya?" Sarah asked, totally charmed.

"An expression my aunt uses," Rashid admitted.

Sarah glanced at the small crevice. "Very American, too."

"Yes. It's a good one." This time when Rashid winked, he managed to flutter only one eye.

Sarah felt the familiar bump in her heart.

"You surprise me, Miss Kwong."

"How?" she asked, her eyes locked on the little boy as he walked a few feet away.

"Rather than a taxi, I thought you'd be more of the 'jump in the fire-red sports convertible' type of person."

The fury whipped through her, split-second fast and razor wicked.

She caught the speed, throttled the anger back. But the wicked broke free and curved her lips. "Actually, I drive a hedonistic black sports convertible. My father's words, not mine.

"But when I step out with it—usually in a fire-red dress—I wear them both with class. Something my father said comes from good breeding and even better manners."

She heard the hiss, a rasp of air caught between clenched jaws but she didn't turn, simply because she didn't care. Maybe it was the fact he'd come close to the mark, or the fact that she'd already spent the day surviving a plane crash and dodging madmen with machine guns. Or maybe she just couldn't understand how a jaded man like Jarek could have such a wonderful little boy like Rashid.

In the end, none of it mattered. Even the possibility of being sent home on the next available flight out of Taer.

"I deserved that," Jarek admitted on a sigh. "I apologize, Sarah. My father raised me better also."

The sincerity caught her, another nudge, but unlike Rashid's remark, Jarek hit her deeper, in the pit of her stomach.

"Apology accepted."

"Thank you," Jarek replied softly, simply. But his gaze, one that had the darkest part of his eyes flaring with awareness, wasn't simple.

And suddenly, being sent home on the next flight from Taer didn't sound so bad to Sarah.

STONES, some the size of adult fists, others small boulders, sprung free from the ledges and tumbled down the walls to the chasm below. But most stayed on the trail, little enough to make their way into Sarah's shoes, dig in her heel and, after an hour or two, rubbed her toes raw.

"We'll stop here for the night."

Jarek halted the horses in front of a shallow crevice. It was identical to many others they had passed along the path.

"Here?" She picked a particularly sharp stone free from beneath the arch of her foot and decided distance was a relative term when traversing rocks and narrow trails.

He gestured just beyond one side of the crevice to a rock that jutted from the cliff wall.

Sarah looked closer and whistled. The stone lip curved back, hiding a cave entrance wide enough to fit each horse. "My first secret passage."

"Mine, too," Rashid said with awe. "Ali Baba and his thieves could have lived in a cave such as this."

"Let's hope they aren't in there now." Jarek took one of the glow sticks from the survival pack. "Sometimes there are lions in the caves, as well as vipers and scorpions. Stay here while I check to make sure it is safe."

Sarah heard the snap of the stick and suddenly the entrance was dimly lit with neon green light.

"So you like Ali Baba, do you?"

"The story is my Aunt Anna's favorite. She reads it to me and my cousin Kadan when we are sick."

"It's clear." Jarek stepped out of the cave and gestured them in with the horses.

Eight foot in height, the crevice opened into a cave more than thirty feet deep and ten feet wide.

"This is huge," Rashid murmured, leading Ping through.

"I don't know about huge," Jarek mused, tugging Taaj forward. "But it will provide protection from the cold."

The scent of stale earth and dust caught in Sarah's throat, making her cough. But it was the dankness of the rocks that made her rub her bare arms.

"Why is it damp?" Sarah forced her eyes to focus through the shadows. "Is there water in here?"

"Yes." He led her to the rear of the cave. A small stream trickled down the back wall into a natural basin of rocks at the floor.

"You've been here before." It was a statement, not a question, but Jarek chose to answer Sarah anyway.

"Quamar and I spent quite a bit of time out here exploring when we were younger." Jarek took a few more of the glow sticks out of the pack, snapped them, then tossed them onto the floor.

"This will have to do for light. We cannot start a fire. The rocks at the entrance would conceal the flames, but not the smoke."

"We should have energy bars or something in the survival kit."

"Rashid, we'll leave the horses saddled, just in case. But I want you to help me bring them back here to drink some water. After, we'll return them to the front of the cave. They'll give us warning if anyone approaches."

"Yes, Papa."

While father and son took care of the animals, Sarah grabbed the backpack and sat down on the ground.

Laughter caught her attention. A rich, deep chuckle that made a woman's breath hitch, her heart beat just a tad faster.

Deliberately, she turned her back to the pair and sorted through the survival kit.

After a while, Rashid joined her at the wall. "Papa's finishing Taaj's feeding bag."

"Are you hungry?"

"Not really," Rashid said, his voice rough with fatigue. He rubbed his eyes. "I had oat cakes while we rode on Taaj."

"Want a place to sleep?" She scooted back, until her back bumped the wall, then patted her legs. "I've heard my lap is pretty comfortable."

Jarek watched from a distance as Rashid snuggled against Sarah.

He was almost too big for her slight frame, but she wrapped her arms around him and managed to tuck his head under her chin.

Within moments, Rashid's body relaxed and his breathing deepened.

"Asleep?" Jarek crouched next to her. His knuckles brushed his son's cheek. "I want to check the perimeter one more time. When you get tired, I'll take him from you."

Surprised at the gentleness in Jarek's voice, Sarah glanced at him. "You're not going to order me to put him down right now?"

Jarek nearly smiled at the suspicion in her voice. Sarah Kwong was no pushover.

"No, not right now."

"What happens next?"

"We wait to see what morning brings." He sat down next to her, stretched his legs out and leaned back against the wall. His muscles flexed, trying to shed the fatigue and the strain from the constant vigilance that had kept them tight for the last twelve hours. "If we have to, we'll circle back to the city or head toward my Uncle's caravan. Either way, I will get us there."

"Can I ask how? The Sahara is almost as large as the continental United States. We can go days without seeing anyone."

"You forget, this is my backyard."

"A backyard that has been infested."

"That's a very good analogy," Jarek replied. "The Al Asheera have scattered, then hide in the sands, like vermin. It makes it difficult to flush them out into the open."

"Have you ever tried rat poison?"

"No, but I might."

"Will your cousin look for you?"

"Yes," Jarek laid his forearm across his eyes. "But still it will take time. Until then we must keep safe."

For the first time that day, she realized she actually did feel safe.

"Who is Roldo, Your Majesty?"

"I have no idea." Jarek didn't open his eyes. "Why?"

"Just before he died, Ramon told me to run from Roldo." She shifted Rashid just a bit to look at Jarek. "He also said to tell you he was sorry."

"Did he say why?"

"No. Actually, he didn't say anything after that. Those were his last words."

Jarek said nothing for a moment. Only the tightening of his fist indicated he'd heard. "Could Ramon have been delirious when he spoke the name?"

"He was aware enough to hand me his gun for protection." Her eyes lingered over his profile while his eyes remained closed. The green hue of light didn't detract from the carved features, but somehow it softened the line of his mouth, the line of his jaw. Just enough to give her a glimpse of where Rashid's boyish features came from.

"Did the Al Asheera think you were on the plane?"

"It's highly likely," Jarek answered. "But even if they didn't. The death or torture of an American reporter would not go well with Jon Mercer's and my diplomatic efforts. The fact that you are his daughter's friend only adds to the prize."

"I didn't get this job because I was Lara's friend," she pointed out.

"If I thought you had, you wouldn't be here," Jarek retorted. This time his mouth twitched with amusement over her quick defense. She was a woman with pride, and maybe a little vanity.

Both were fine if well deserved. And from what he'd seen of Sarah Kwong's files, both were deserved.

"The president holds a tremendous amount of respect for you."

The primness in the tone, made Jarek open his eyes.

"But you don't." Jarek turned his head until he faced her. Without thinking, she rubbed her cheek against Rashid's temple. "My opinion isn't the question here."

It had been a long time since a woman had held his son. Even Anna didn't come near as much anymore, Jarek realized. Emotion raced through him.

"No. Just my integrity, it seems," Jarek responded. "Tell me, is your low opinion simply because I did not meet you in Morocco?"

"No," she admitted. When her hair fell in a curtain over his son's shoulder and neck, she automatically brushed it back. "I tend not to trust people who keep secrets. It comes with the job."

"And you believe I have a secret."

"No, Your Majesty. I believe you have many secrets."

"You're wrong." Jarek gave into his urge and captured several strands of hair from her shoulder. He rubbed them between his forefinger and thumb, enjoying its cool, silky texture. "You see it's not what I am hiding. It's what I am protecting."

He glanced down at his son. "Although it seems I haven't done a good job with that, either."

Chapter Five

Roldo Costa sat on the jeep's hood, anger twisting his insides into a vicious knot. It wasn't his fault the king and his brat slipped past Oruk's men. He dug into his pocket for his paper and bag of weed.

Hell, it wasn't his job to search and destroy.

It was only to destroy, Roldo thought with contempt.

But then, the Al Asheera leader never appreciated the beauty of Roldo's expertise.

Effortlessly, he rolled the joint and licked the paper closed. The desert chill had settled in, making his mood even fouler. He wanted to be at the city's brothel, a place called the Cathouse, drinking and whoring.

The women liked him there. They thought he was a big shot because he got them booze from Milan and drugs from a cousin in Columbia.

They thought he was tough, too.

He lit the joint and took a long drag. The smoke was harsh, spurred by the cocaine he'd added to the mix. It bit at the back of his throat, burned its way to his chest.

While he waited to catch his buzz, Roldo pulled his Glock from his shoulder holster, enjoying the weight of it in his hand.

Since the jeep had no roof, he reached over the windshield of the jeep and flipped on the headlights.

A buzzard squawked, its wings flapping against the stark beams. But it didn't fly away. It wasn't willing to give up its meal of rotted flesh unless it was absolutely sure there was danger near.

Roldo leveled his pistol at the bird. "Take off, you dumb son of a bitch. Fly while you can."

The bird stared at him for a moment, then settled back into his meal.

"Stupid bird." Roldo squeezed the trigger. Laughing at the puff of feathers, he watched the vulture flop dead.

He shoved his gun back into its holster, took another hit off his joint. "Let's see if the Royals are as stupid as you, bird," he yelled. He left the joint hanging from the corner of his mouth and walked around to the back of the jeep.

From the boot, he pulled out C-4, a detonator and wire. "This is the difference between smart and stupid, bird," he muttered.

Like the vultures, Oruk's men tracked their prey, and then waited for it to drop dead in front of them.

Stupid.

Roldo, on the other hand, set the trap, added the right bait, then let the prey come to him. He flicked the joint nub into the sand and ground it under his heel.

Smart.

Confident, he counted off paces from the jeep to the plane. If he hurried, he'd still have time for a few drinks at the cantina.

Smiling at the thought, he stepped over the bird and got to work.

"HOW HAVE YOU BEEN, Sarah?" The question broke through the silence that had filled the cave for the past hour.

"Good," she said cautiously, unsure from where the question came. They had just put Rashid down on a make-shift bed of the emergency blanket and Jarek's robe.

"And your father and mother, how are they?"

Slowly, Sarah finished tucking the robe around Rashid's shoulders and straightened. "They are doing well.

"My father has retired from the university," she added. "They are currently traveling in a motor home somewhere in Yellowstone National Park. I get e-mails when they have access to the Internet, and postcards when they don't." She paused for a moment. "But I assume you already know that, since the president sent you my file."

"He told you?"

"The first time I met with him over the possibility of flying to Taer, he told me his intentions," Sarah mused. "Should I be flattered that you took such an interest in me after all these years?"

"Before I made an agreement with Jon Mercer, I had your background checked."

"And you're telling me this, why?" Sarah asked. "Considering you're a king and run your own country, I don't think you need to reach for the intimidation card. So why share this information with me now?"

"I will not let just anyone into my home, Sarah. Even on the recommendation of a president."

"Especially past lovers," Sarah added. When Jarek didn't respond—didn't deny her statement—Sarah brushed the hurt aside.

"Fair enough," she said and meant it. After all, she'd researched him, too. "So you're telling me, I'm on probation."

"I'm telling you that just because we are in this situation here, it will not change the situation once we reach the city again."

"Okay," Sarah replied slowly. "I stand warned."

"Come sit over here." Jarek dug into the backpack and retrieved the first aid kit. "We need to clean the cut on your forehead. And your feet. Infection sets in relatively easy in the desert."

"I can do it."

"How? When I can see it better than you?" he mused, his lips tilting, challenging her reluctance. "You're not afraid, are you?"

Of you, yes. "Of a little pain? No," she retorted, deliberately misunderstanding his question.

She sat cross-legged on the ground. But when he crouched in front of her, she tensed.

"Relax," he murmured, in the same even tone he'd used on the horses.

While her features remained passive, she could do very little to ease the tension in her shoulders.

For the first few minutes, Jarek worked in silence, cleaning the cut with an antiseptic wipe.

"This will sting."

Sarah hissed at the sharp slice of pain. "You weren't kidding."

Gently, he blew across the wound, taking the sting away from her temple. "I never realized you had graduated from the University of Nevada."

"Forty-eight hours doesn't allow much time for much personal history." But was plenty of time to fall in love with a king, she thought.

"The file said you graduated at the top of your class. Majored in journalism. Minored in history." Jarek brushed away a few strands of hair, tucked them behind her ear. "That must have made your father happy."

"It did." The brush of his finger against the shell of her ear touched off a ripple of goose bumps down her neck. "But I happen to enjoy history. So it made me happy, too."

"You are quite brave, Sarah," he said, his voice dropping to a husky murmur. His fingers worked efficiently. His feather-light touches were gentle, almost soothing as he applied the medicated cream.

"Not really." Without realizing it, her voice dipped low to match his. "I've had worse injuries."

With him only mere inches away, it was hard not to study the man. The set plains of his face, the jaw slightly dusted with whiskers, the sculpted line of his mouth.

This wasn't the man who ruled a country. It was the man who haunted her dreams.

"I'm not talking about this cut," Jarek explained and reached for a butterfly bandage. "You've weathered the day pretty well, considering."

"I guess," she whispered, closing her eyes against the brush of his knuckle against her cheek. "One doesn't have a choice in a situation like this."

He pressed the small bandage to her temple. "I've known many who've acted cowardly under less dangerous situations."

"Then you might want to question the company you keep." Suddenly, she remembered she was addressing royalty. "I'm sorry, Your Majesty."

"No need to be sorry. I happen to agree with you. But sometimes we are not able to choose so easily." Jarek placed another bandage on her wound. "You might have a scar."

"It's just a mark," she joked, but the words were no

more than a whisper. "And it isn't the first. In third grade, I got into a fight with the playground bully. It wasn't pretty."

"Did he hurt you?" His fingers drifted over the delicate line of her jaw.

"It was a girl," she joked lightly. "And I gave her a fat lip. But walked away with a nasty scar on my shin. She was wearing roller skates. The metal kind."

"You're pretty tough aren't you?" His thumb skimmed the soft skin behind her ear.

"Sometimes." In that moment, the lightness was lost, destroyed by the shiver that tripped down her spine, the tension that curled tight in her belly. "Then, other times, not very tough at all."

"How about now?" Jarek's gaze drifted over her features, rested for a moment on her mouth.

"Papa?"

Jarek stiffened. His hand dropped away from her face. "I'm here. Go back to sleep, son."

"Yes, Papa."

After the little boy turned over, Jarek stood. "Sarah, I—"

"Don't," she said quickly, then untucked her hair from her ear, using the long strands as a curtain to cover her confusion. "It's all right. We both got carried away." She tried for flippancy, but managed a quiet sort of dignity. "We'll chalk it up to the stress of day."

"Time to sleep, then."

"Together?" Her head shot up.

"With Rashid between us," Jarek corrected. "Trust me, he is a ball of heat. You just have to watch the elbows and knees."

"I have nieces that are the same age." Sarah slipped off

her shoes and placed them in her purse. "I take it he's crawled in bed with you on occasion."

Jarek glanced from Sarah to the sleeping boy. So many things had slipped away. "He used to."

Chapter Six

Memories took their revenge in the subconscious, spurred by the vulnerability that came with sleep. The thwack of the whip against raw flesh. The whimpers of the almost dead. The dull rhythmic beat of both sounds swirled and ebbed—a backbeat to his nightmare. Seductive, persuasive, both whispered to him, nurtured by the dark edge of insanity, the bitterness of betrayal.

When he fought back, the demons came. They ripped through his skin, splaying muscle and bone, exposing nerves until the air turned foul—thick with the stench of rancid blood and feces.

Jarek awoke, his jaw clenched, sweat sticking between his shirt and skin. He cursed the memories, the scars on his back that would never let him forget.

A penance for past sins.

It was rare for Jarek to sleep more than a few hours a night. Even rarer for the nightmares to leave him in peace.

Unaware of his demons, Sarah continued sleeping, her head resting in the crook of Jarek's shoulder.

Rashid lay between them, his head pillowed against her chest and one arm flung over her side.

A shaft of longing speared his chest, catching him off-guard.

The horses shifted, their stance turned edgy. Taaj blew air out of his nostrils in warning.

Slowly Jarek untangled himself from Rashid and Sarah.

When she stirred, he placed a hand over her mouth. "Quiet," he whispered. "We've got company. Wake Rashid."

When she nodded, he grabbed his rifle from the wall nearby. "Ramon's gun is in the backpack," he said almost tonelessly.

Sarah nodded again, this time the movement was stiff with fear.

"Be careful," she whispered.

But he was gone.

Quickly, she put her hand to Rashid's mouth and shook his shoulder. "Wake up, sport."

SHADOWS STRETCHED and twisted beyond the cave and into the semidarkness. The chill of the night lingered in the cool and damp of the predawn.

Taaj moved restlessly against Jarek. "It's all right, my friend," he murmured, adding a few words in his native tongue of Taer.

After the animals settled, he followed the wall to the edge of the cave opening.

The noise was soft. A whisper of cloth against stone. The grind of sand beneath a heel.

But it was enough.

Soundlessly, Jarek placed his rifle against the wall and drew his knife from his boot.

The shadows stretched farther—morphing suddenly into the shape of a man's head and shoulders.

Jarek waited the length of a three heartbeats, then stepped out from the rocks, knife first.

The man, startled, let out a whoosh of breath as the knife made contact with his first rib. Jarek lifted and shoved. The man hit the wall, his eyes frozen, his face nothing more than a mask of death. Slowly, Jarek stepped back, then froze when he heard a faint bleep.

He glanced down at the man's wrist and caught the green glow of a miniature GPS receiver. Quickly he cut the device from the rebel's wrist and shoved it into his pocket.

Suddenly, another man jumped from the path. Younger, than the first, his eyes wide in fear. The rebel raised his rifle and fired. Three shots exploded into the night air, before Jarek's knife found its mark in the man's chest.

Swearing, Jarek reached for the watch in his pocket. The signal in his hand grew stronger as he returned to the cave.

"What is it, Papa?"

Jarek didn't answer, instead he ripped the gun from Sarah's hand and tossed it to the ground.

"What are you doing? Are you crazy?"

"How much did they pay you, Miss Kwong?"

"What are you talking about—"

Jarek grabbed her purse and dumped it onto the floor. The wristband suddenly vibrated against his fingers.

"You didn't have time to tell them I wasn't on the plane with you?" He reached down and grabbed a small round disc from the pile of items. He smashed it under his heel. The vibration stopped. "They must have promised a lot of money for you to risk your life in a plane crash."

"You're delusional. I have no idea how that tracking bug got into my purse," Sarah argued. "For all you know, Ramon—"

"Don't!" Fury flashed crossed Jarek's features. He grabbed her arm and jerked her forward.

"Try it," Sarah warned, her own anger flaring. She met him toe-to-toe. The sting of accusation drove any thought of fear from her mind. "That bug could've been put in my purse by anyone, anywhere. You've just been waiting for an excuse to ship me home."

"I'm not sending you home anytime soon. You're going to be my personal guest until I decide what to do with you."

"Personal guest?" Sarah seethed. "You mean a prisoner, don't you?"

"Call it what you want."

When she turned on her heel, he grabbed her arm, forcing her back around.

"Don't you dare touch me, you son of a—"

"Papa?"

Sarah snapped her teeth together, but her glare didn't waver.

"Get your things, Rashid. We need to leave." Jarek's tone was short, uncompromising. "The Al Asheera will find us. And when they do, we'll be cornered if we don't move."

Startled, Sarah argued. "It's too dark—"

"The sun will rise within an hour. A blessing and a curse. We will have better footing, but we will also become easier targets."

Jarek released his hold. "Gather your belongings."

Angry, she picked up her things and shoved them back into her purse. "I hope you have a plan. Or are you planning on spending the next few days roaming these cliffs."

"We will find my uncle's caravan."

"Uncle Bari?" Rashid asked, frowning.

"Yes."

"But Taaj. And Ping?"

"We leave the horses and continue on foot." Jarek grabbed Ramon's pistol from the ground, then shoved it into the backpack. "I am familiar with these paths. We should have no problems navigating them for the short time before dawn breaks over the horizon."

"And if we fall?"

"We won't. The ledges are dangerous, but can be traveled," Jarek commented grimly. "And we have little choice. Those shots you heard were a signal. It will be only a matter of time before more of your friends pinpoint our location."

Sarah refused to defend herself again.

"If we leave the horses, they could die," Rashid insisted while he blocked the entrance, his hands fisted.

"Where we have to go, the ledges are too narrow for them to maneuver." Jarek slipped the backpack straps over his shoulders. "By my estimates, Bari's caravan is less than two days west of here if we cut through the cliff faces. Once we reach the caravan, I will make sure the horses will be taken care of."

"Two days without food—"

"As long as they have the water from the spring they can go two days without food." This time he didn't disguise the impatience in his tone. "Do not worry, Rashid. Taaj will take care of Ping."

"Yes, Papa." The young boy held back a small sob and went to say goodbye to his horse.

"If Ping dies, Rashid will never forgive himself," Sarah warned Jarek quietly.

"Better a horse than my son," Jarek snapped back, barely managing to keep his voice low. "Damn it. He should not have been out here. He should not have followed me."

"Maybe you should not have ridden out here, either."

"If I hadn't you'd be a prisoner of the Al Asheera."

"Better me than your son." Using his words against him. "Of course, I could be conspiring with them."

"I hope for your sake the latter is true."

"And why is that?"

"I have seen firsthand how the Al Asheera torture women."

Chapter Seven

When they stepped outside the cave, the predawn haze blurred the line of day and night, leaving most of the area still in shadows.

"I hope you have an excellent memory, Your Majesty."

"The sun will soon break over the horizon, then we will have more light." Within moments, the path narrowed to less than three feet, drawing the edge of the cliff closer. Jarek had no choice but to place Rashid between him and Sarah.

"Watch your step. The edge crumbles without notice," Jarek warned. He slipped off the backpack and held it in front of him. "Keep your back pressed to the wall whenever possible."

"You're kidding right?"

Rashid found her hand with his and squeezed. "We will be all right, Sarah—"

A shot pinged off the rock near Rashid's face. She stifled a scream and gripped the boy closer to her side.

Jarek swore. "Looks like the Al Asheera turned on you, Miss Kwong."

A shout came from below the ridge as more fire peppered the walls above them.

Jarek dropped the backpack and quickly pulled Rashid

under a slight overhang. "Stay with Sarah under the ledge and close to the wall."

He pinned her with his stare. "Keep him safe. Or so help me—"

More gunfire exploded above their heads. "Where is safe?" she muttered while Jarek made his way farther down the path.

"Papa?" Rashid took a step toward his father.

"Stay there! You're protected by the overhang," he ordered sharply. "No matter what happens, do not move."

"Jarek!" Sarah pointed up.

Thirty men lined the ridge a hundred feet above them, their crimson robes easily seen against the backdrop of the morning sky.

Jarek fired his rifle. Sarah heard a scream, then a volley of gunfire pounded the path close to her and Rashid.

"If you give yourself up, we will not harm your son," a man called from the ridge.

"Jarek?" Sarah glanced down at Rashid. They were pinned to the wall. Easy targets for the men above.

"Don't follow!" he shouted at Sarah. "Or so help me—"

Suddenly a rocket exploded behind the group of men. Screams ricocheted and bodies tumbled from the rocks into the ravine below.

The *whop-whop* of helicopter blades filled the chasm, until the buzz numbed the air around them. Two helicopters hovered into Jarek's view. Each with the symbol of the Taer military on its belly.

"It's Uncle Quamar!" Excited, the little boy stepped away from the wall to wave.

"Rashid!" But Sarah's warning came too late.

Machine gunfire burst from the first helicopter, driving the Al Asheera back, knocking the stones from the wall.

The overhang broke loose with a shudder, catching the little boy in its path.

Sarah threw herself to the ground and reached for Rashid's hand just as he disappeared over the edge.

"I have you." Sarah held tight to Rashid's hands, leaving his body dangling over the gully beneath.

"Sarah! Help!" The little boy screamed. "My hands are slipping."

"Hold on, sweetheart." She lay awkwardly along the path with half her body over the edge. Rocks scraped her belly, dug into her ribs. She tried to shift back, to give herself leverage, but the ledge left her no room to maneuver. "Jarek!"

She didn't dare look up to find him, so instead she stayed focused on Rashid's head. "Hurry. I don't know how long I can hold him."

She could feel the sweat gather in her palms, her fingers cramp under the added weight. Terror whipped through her, making her limbs shake.

"Almost there." The path had fallen away, leaving Jarek stranded on the other side. He studied the four-foot gap and the surrounding area, made his decision in a millisecond.

With his back to the wall, Jarek straddled the gap, placing his foot softly, testing the other side of the path. Finding it solid, he shifted his weight across the missing portion of the ledge.

Twisting, Rashid tried to find footing in the rock. The movement jarred Sarah's shoulders.

"Stay still," she ordered, her voice sharp.

Immediately, Rashid froze, letting his feet dangle once more.

"Jarek!" Sarah's arms shook, the muscles straining to hold the little boy. Once again, she tried shifting back but the leverage wasn't there.

She caught a slight movement out of the corner of her eye.

"Sarah! Scorpion!" Rashid screamed the warning. Sarah cried out because the little boy squirmed, jerking her neck, weakening her grip.

Without warning, the sting hit her forearm and set her whole limb on fire.

"Hang on, Sarah."

Sarah looked down at her arm. The skin on her forearm swelled. "Hurry, Jarek, I can't feel my hand."

"I'm here." Jarek laid on top of her and reached for Rashid. He hauled the boy up to him. Within moments, Jarek had Sarah and his son in his arms.

He held them both for a long minute, trying to get his own heart rate under control.

"Keep your arm lower than your heart." Jarek shifted Rashid next to him on the ledge. "Don't move again," he warned his son.

He ripped two long strips of material from his scarf.

Jarek tied one strip above and one just below the sting on Sarah's arm.

"What do we do?" Rashid asked, his voice tight with fear. With shaking hands, Jarek gathered his son and Sarah back under his arms. "Now we wait for your Uncle Quamar."

He glanced down at Sarah. "Thank you."

"You're welcome."

"Hello, Sarah."

Quamar Al Asadi was a big man, over six feet of solid muscle with a bald head and a gentle smile that reached warm, brown eyes.

"Hello, Quamar." Sarah smiled ruefully. "I was hoping to see you under better circumstances."

He clasped her hands in his big, meaty palms, then took his time looking at her injury. "It is no more than a scratch," he teased, before he leaned in and kissed her forehead. "You are okay?"

"Yes."

"Do you know each other?" Jarek asked, even as his eyes rested on his son.

Rashid hadn't left Sarah's side since they'd been rescued.

"Yes, Your Majesty, we have mutual friends. Ian and Lara MacAlister."

"Ian. I'd forgotten." Jarek frowned. "Did you find the plane?"

"No," the giant answered after a moment. "But if you have the coordinates—"

"Ramon is dead, Quamar. We will retrieve his body at the first opportunity. But first I want to make sure everything is secure at the palace."

Jarek's words were even, emotionless. But Quamar knew his cousin better than anyone. The loss of Ramon would've hit Jarek hard, but as in the manner of the king, he would grieve in private.

"Understandable," Quamar replied, his voice hushed as Rashid darted from Sarah to his father's side. Already from the smiles, the soft pat of her hand on the child's face, Quamar could see a unit formed between the three. He just didn't know yet if it was a good thing.

"Sarah saved me, Uncle Quamar."

"Yes, she did," Quamar confirmed, his voice low, and just raspy enough to show the fear that still lingered inside him. It had taken them a half an hour to get the three of them off of the ledge and onto flat ground. A half an hour in which Quamar's soldiers chased off the remaining Al Asheera rebels.

"The rocks came down and hit me. I lost my balance and went over the side."

"And Sarah caught you?"

"Yes." Rashid held up both his hands where bruises dotted his wrists. "She didn't let go even when the scorpion stung her."

"She is a hero." Quamar stood beside his nephew, his own hands folded behind his back to cover their trembling. "If it were me, I would have saved you simply so I could lecture you about scaring myself and your Aunt Anna half to death with your disappearance."

"But my note told you where to find me," Rashid said, but he could not hold his uncle's gaze.

"Yes, it did. Just in time, too," Quamar agreed, then tipped his nephew's chin up with a gentle finger. "And for that, we are all very grateful."

"Aunt Sandra!"

Quamar and Jarek turned in unison. A woman, dressed efficiently in khaki cotton trousers and a short-sleeved blouse, approached. She was petite, looked to be no more than thirty years old with a short cap of dark hair that feathered at the ends.

"Hi, handsome." Dr. Sandra Haddad hugged Rashid to her. "Are you okay? Any concussions?" Sandra studied Rashid's eyes for a moment.

"He's fine," Quamar responded for his nephew.

"Your Majesty." Sandra opted out of the formal courtesy and instead, slightly bowed her head.

"You're quite a ways from your clinic, Sandra." Jarek stepped forward and gave her a hug. "But I'm certainly glad to see you."

"Sandra was out in the field when we heard the news. I radioed her helicopter pilot with your location." Quamar stepped back and gestured to Sarah. "Sarah Kwong, this is Doctor Sandra Haddad. Her father, Omar, is Taer's main physician. Sandra grew up with us here. Sandra, Sarah battled a scorpion."

"Unfortunately, there is little we can do for a scorpion bite," Sandra responded, setting down a black medical bag near Sarah.

"Death Stalkers are the most poisonous in the desert," Rashid commented. "Isn't that right, Aunt Sandra?"

"Yes, they are." She took a syringe from her bag along with a few antiseptic wipes. "This is going to hurt, Miss Kwong."

"More than the sting does?" Sarah asked jokingly.

"Possibly," Sandra admitted with a twitch to her lips.

"Then I guess you'd better call me Sarah. Because if it hurts too much, I might be calling you other names besides Doctor."

Sandra laughed, a deep feminine chuckle that had both men glancing their way. "I'll give you something to take the edge off the pain in a minute."

"Anyone who can joke over pain will live a while longer," Quamar commented wryly to Jarek. Then he caught his cousin's face, the firm set of his jaw. He understood what both meant. "This wasn't your fault, Jarek. If anything, you saved her from a horrible death. A sting from a scorpion is easier to survive than the strike of an Al Asheera sword."

"The pain will stay with her for a day or so," Jarek murmured. "They bugged her purse. Either with or without her consent."

While they watched, Sandra wound a white bandage around Sarah's arm, then tied the material off.

"So the next time you want a morning to yourself, take a

satellite phone and GPS unit with you," Quamar reasoned. "I will not have to rely on a smoke signal to find you."

"I injected a synthetic anti venom," Sandra interrupted. "Then gave her a sedative to help with the pain. She still needs to spend the night in the hospital for observation. Scorpion stings tend to cause nausea and fevers."

"Not the hospital. The palace," Jarek ordered, then in a lower voice he added, "I want a twenty-four-hour watch on her."

Quamar raised his eyebrow, but said nothing.

"Send some men to the northeast peak. We left the horses in a cave there. The one with the spring and rock trough."

"I will. I'll have the pilot radio ahead to the palace." Quamar looked at Sarah. "You will be well taken care of."

"ONE HUNDRED AND ONE," Sandra observed and pulled the thermometer from Sarah's ear. She popped off the plastic cover into a nearby wastebasket. "Still a little high. But with rest you should be fine. No more tangling with scorpions."

"Deal." Sarah grimaced against the ache in her muscles and bones. Slowly she eased back into goose-down bed pillows.

True to his word, Jarek had her delivered to one of the royal suites in the palace. Although she hadn't seen more than the king-size bed covered and canopied in mixtures of dark claret and pale roses, the soft decadent combination of satin and cotton were nothing less than heavenly after two days in the desert.

"You know, we met about four years ago. At one of your Las Vegas seminars on synthetic viruses."

"Really?" Sandra picked up the water pitcher from the table and poured some into a glass.

"I was in a mob of reporters."

"I'm sure to remember you now," she teased and handed Sarah two pills and a glass of water. "Take these. They will help you sleep."

"I doubt I'll need much help." Even with Sandra's assistance, it had taken Sarah more than an hour to get cleaned up and put back to bed. Once she was there, the exhaustion took over. "Can I ask you a question?"

"Sure."

"You had quite a reputation a few years back. One that extended out of your research. Then all of a sudden, you dropped off the radar. Why?"

"Sometimes a job can consume a person," Sandra answered easily. "Mine was one of them. So I decided to take a break."

"I see." Instinctively, Sarah believed there was more to the story, but she decided to let it go.

"You'll have a slight fever for the next twenty-four hours and your arm will hurt for a few days. Keep it bandaged to avoid infection and after today, take aspirin for the pain. The swelling should be down by the morning."

Sandra placed her stethoscope in her bag and snapped it shut. "I have to say, I'm glad you're the one who was stung. If that scorpion had gotten to Rashid, he'd be in a much more serious position now. Children cannot fight the venom as well."

"Hello, Auntie Sandra!" Rashid rushed in and threw himself at Sandra.

"Hello again, handsome." Sandra caught him against her legs and gave him a hug. "How are you?"

"Good." Rashid pulled away and sat on the bed, his hands hidden behind his back. "Sarah, Uncle Quamar saved Taaj and Ping. He said other than being hungry, they were no worse for their adventure."

"I'm glad, Rashid. Very glad."

"Does it hurt?"

Sarah opted for a portion of the truth. "Some, but nothing like earlier."

"I'll give her some medicine that will make the pain go away for a while."

"I'm glad." Rashid smiled, his hands still behind his back. "Uncle Quamar says you are a hero and should be acknowledged at the Independence Ball, the day after tomorrow."

"I don't think—"

"He said he's going to talk to Papa about it. After all, you saved the Prince of Taer." Rashid pointed his thumb at his chest and giggled. "I'm important, you know."

Sarah laughed. "Yes, you are."

Sandra kissed his forehead. "I think that you had better start figuring out how you're going to explain your actions to your father, now that you're home safe and sound."

"Do you think he'll forget?" Rashid's small eyebrows drew together. "Papa has been very busy since we've been back."

"I seriously doubt it, Rashid," Sarah said, silently adding it would take a long time for her to forget that kind of fear.

Sandra caught her gaze knowingly. "So, young man, what are you hiding?"

"A book." Rashid pulled it out from behind his back. "*Ali Baba and the Forty Thieves.*"

"The story your Aunt Anna always reads to you when you're sick," Sarah remembered.

"It always makes me feel better."

"It's Anna's favorite, isn't it, Rashid," Sandra acknowledged. "She even has a camel named Morgiana."

"The slave girl from the book," Sarah inserted.

"Yes," Sandra replied. She took the book from Rashid

and flipped through the worn pages. "Quamar calls the animal Anna's pet. She's had it since—"

"Since she saved me from certain death when I was a baby," Rashid interrupted. He climbed up next to Sarah's side. "That's what Uncle Quamar says."

"And that is exactly what happened." Sandra ruffled the young boy's hair.

Suddenly shy, he asked Sarah, "Would you like me to read to you and see if you feel better, too?"

Tears pricked Sarah's eyes. If she hadn't loved the little boy already, she would've fallen in that instant. She put her good arm around him and hugged him close. "I would like that very much."

"Then I'll leave you both to it." Sandra picked up her bag and kissed the young prince on the forehead. "Just don't stay too long, Rashid. Even heroes need their rest."

"SO ARE YOU GOING TO TELL ME how you know Sarah Kwong?" Quamar asked as he shut the office door to allow Jarek and him more privacy.

"Why are you so sure that I do?" Jarek leaned back in his chair and looked at the giant across from his desk. They'd grown up together, more brothers than cousins. Jarek trusted no other as much, besides his Uncle Bari, and understood no other could read him better. Still, the fact Quamar had noticed anything rubbed him wrong.

"I have seen the way you look at her." Quamar waved a dismissive hand. "And others will, too, if you do not take care."

Jarek sighed. "I met Sarah eight years ago in New York at a political affair hosted by President Robert Cambridge. A few years before Jon Mercer took office. She and her father, Dr. Shen Kwong, attended."

"Anna's father," Quamar murmured, trying to place the name. "I seem to remember that he and your father were good friends."

"Yes. Dr. Kwong is a well-known professor of history. He won the Pulitzer prize for his work on the early Chinese migration to the United States quite a few years ago," Jarek replied. "My father had a passion for history. It was only a matter of time before they crossed paths."

"Small world," Quamar commented. "My mother worked with Dr. Kwong several times." Theresa Bazan, Quamar's mother, was a well-known, Pulitzer-winning, Italian photo journalist who had died years before at the hands of the Al Asheera. "I can remember her speaking highly of him."

"I accompanied my parents to New York and attended the ball. Robert Cambridge introduced me to Sarah and her parents that night," Jarek continued, shrugging. "I ran into Sarah alone later that evening on the balcony. One night turned into a romantic weekend."

"And?"

"And nothing. I discovered she was a journalist and so I left."

"Simple enough," Quamar said wryly. "And mutual, I take it?"

"No," Jarek admitted with some reluctance. "I was angry she hadn't told me, so I became…unavailable once I returned to Taer."

Quamar grunted. "Not your most diplomatic moment."

"At the time, it was more than I figured she deserved."

"That's not like you, Jarek. You do not become judge and jury without getting all of the facts."

"This was different somehow," Jarek acknowledged for the first time. "She was different."

"You were falling in love with her."

"No. Nothing liked that," Jareḳ denied. "But I had expected the newspapers to be filled with articles of our affair."

"And were they?"

"No." Jarek lifted a casual shoulder. "But my father was still alive at the time and Taer did not become well-known until a few years later when we discovered the oil. I assumed her story got buried."

"Or there might never have been a story."

"It doesn't matter either way," Jarek stated. "Later that same year, I met Saree and we married."

"So Saree was your rebound from Sarah," Quamar surmised. "Fate does have a certain way of interfering with love does it not?"

"I did not love Sarah, Quamar." But the doubt was there, mocking him.

Quamar ignored the denial. "Out of curiosity. Who told you Sarah was a journalist?"

Jarek stiffened. "Hassan."

Their uncle, Hassan, had been killed during the rebellion. But only after Jarek and Quamar had discovered he was the traitor behind the uprising.

"You're suggesting that Hassan wanted my marriage with Saree to take place, so he sabotaged my affair with Sarah."

"As I said," Quamar murmured. "Small world."

"You saw the reaction the people gave Sarah as they brought her from the plane. Do you remember anything close to that kind of loyalty toward Saree?"

"Saree did not save her son from a cliff."

"No, she only gave birth to him."

"Damn it, Quamar. Enough," Jarek snapped. "Is there anything else you wanted discussed?"

"Yes." Quamar accepted that he had pushed his cousin almost too far. It was time for a small retreat to let Jarek think about their conversation.

"Anna and the children are leaving for Washington in two days. Right after the Independence Day Ball."

Ever since Anna and Quamar had married, Anna had acted as Jarek's official hostess for most of Taer's formal events.

"Anna would also like to know if Sarah's stay has been extended. And if she will be attending the ball?"

"Yes," Jarek answered, frowning. "I can't see any way of not inviting her now that she is a local hero."

Quamar's lips twitched with amusement. "You have been speaking with Rashid."

"No, I heard it from everyone Rashid has talked to. Including Anna."

"She can't wait to meet Sarah," Quamar commented. "The only reason why she hasn't yet, is because Sandra had wanted Sarah to rest first."

"And has she?"

"Yes, but only after Rashid read her a story."

"He did?" Jarek frowned.

"It is harmless, Jarek." Quamar reassured him. "Anna reads *Ali Baba* to the children when they are sick. Rashid is only doing what he knows."

Jarek nodded, but it was obvious he didn't like the bond forming between his son and the reporter. "You have told no one of Anna and the children's flight plan, right?"

"Right. Neither has Anna. It will not be hard. The plane is always ready in case of emergencies, so I will have no problem flying out without being seen until it is too late. And I will keep the aircraft at a high altitude.

"I have a friend meeting us in Morocco with his leer

jet," Quamar added. "From there Anna will fly to the United States with the children, and I will return here."

"Make sure Anna does not discuss her plans with Sarah when she visits."

"I will. But I do not agree that Sarah is behind the plane crash," Quamar stated with quiet strength. "Do you really think she would have risked her own life with that tracking device, simply to take yours?"

"She is either the victim or the villain."

"A villain who saved your son," Quamar commented.

"We've just discussed the fact that we've been betrayed before. By those who supposedly loved Rashid," Jarek stated, his voice emotionless. "If the Al Asheera found out the flight times and planted the device, they had help from someone here inside the palace."

"As your advisor, I would suggest Sarah is made a priority, not the enemy. Just for the time she is here. In this case, bad publicity might hurt our diplomatic relations with the United States."

"What do you suggest, that she accompanies me everywhere?"

"That would be best. Leave her in the royal guest suite. The rooms are far enough apart to keep any rumors from starting, but close enough if the necessity rises, Your Majesty."

"You call me 'Your Majesty' only when we are in public or when you are reminding me of my position."

"And we are not in public," Quamar admitted, then sighed. "We both were trained as soldiers, Jarek. You are qualified to keep an eye on her."

Jarek studied his cousin for a moment. "I will consider it."

Quamar nodded, hiding his smile until he turned away.

It wasn't going to be easy, but this might be what Jarek needed to be whole again.

"Where is she?"

"In her room. Safe," Quamar said, his eyebrow raised. "I have posted two guards outside her door."

"Which two?"

"Bash and Ivan."

Jarek nodded. They were seasoned guards having survived the rebellion five years before. "She has been here less than two days and she is already a problem."

"She saved your son," Quamar repeated. "Some would say it is destiny."

Jarek sighed. "Yes, she did. But destiny had nothing to do with it. Jon Mercer did."

"Destiny…" Quamar said, amused "…sometimes needs a little help."

Chapter Eight

"Sarah?"

Startled, Sarah turned over to see Rashid at the bottom of her bed. "Rashid, what time is it?"

"It is almost midnight," the little boy whispered. "I had a bad dream. With scorpions. Elephant scorpions."

"That is bad." Sarah opened the covers and patted the bed next to her.

Rashid slid under and cuddled close. Sarah tried not to give into the love that tightened her heart.

"How did you get in my room?"

"If I tell you, will you keep it our secret?"

"Yes," she agreed, smiling into his hair.

"Through the laundry vent."

"The laundry vent?" She pulled back and studied his face. "Do you mean the chute in the bathroom?"

"Yes," Rashid admitted. "One time Uncle Quamar told me of how his friend, a tiny thief, saved Aunt Anna's life by climbing up the laundry vent. I decided to try it myself."

"How long have you been doing this?"

"Since my last birthday sometime," he confessed. "There is one in every bathroom in the palace. It's easy."

"And convenient," Sarah summarized. "That's how you know so much of what is going on in the palace, isn't it?"

"Yes," Rashid acknowledged reluctantly. "You will not tell my papa, will you?"

She tugged his hair. "No. It's still our secret. But only because the way you're growing, you won't be able to fit in the chute after a few more months."

"Sarah, why don't you like my papa?"

"I don't dislike your father. We are just not close friends."

The little boy nodded, sighing. "My papa does not have any friends. Only Uncle Quamar and Aunt Anna. And me. And my mama, before she died."

"It isn't because your father isn't likable, Rashid. It's just that he's..." She struggled for a word.

"King?" When Sarah nodded, the boy sighed. "Yes, I know."

"He has duties."

"Sarah, do you want to be a mama someday?"

"Yes," she answered carefully, suddenly feeling she was walking a tight rope. "When the time is right."

"Could it be right now?"

Sarah hugged Rashid, wishing with all her heart it could be. "I don't think so."

"Can we be friends, then?"

"We are friends," Sarah said quietly. "The best of friends."

"I don't have many friends, either. I guess that is because I will be king someday."

"Maybe, you'll be a different kind of king."

JAREK CLIMBED the main staircase and loosened his tie. The country didn't suspend itself while he was on the run in the desert.

Schedules had to be adjusted. Trips delayed. Meetings pushed back into the late hours of the night.

Never had he complained. Never had he wished to be something other than what he was. Not even on those days, he found himself less than deserving to bear the responsibility of thousands of lives.

The desert had been Jarek's one freedom. A place to gather his thoughts, seek some peace, if only for a while.

But that had changed.

No longer could he ride the sand, watch the sunset without Sarah's image following him.

Jarek pushed his thoughts away. And, as was his nightly habit, he stopped at Rashid and Kadan's nursery. He nodded to the guards on either side.

Soundless, he opened the door and stepped into the boys' bedroom.

The moonlight spilled through the arched window and across the nursery beds.

At four, Kadan still slept sideways on the bed with his blanket bunched underneath him and his bottom up in the air.

He took a minute and readjusted his nephew, gave him a kiss on the forehead, then walked over to Rashid's bed.

Fear spiked through him. The blankets were rumpled but the bed was empty. Quickly, he walked to the bathroom and flicked on the light. Finding it empty, he started to yell for the guards only to snap his jaw closed.

A note lay folded on Rashid's nightstand.

Jarek snatched it up and read his son's handwriting. Swearing silently, he stalked out of the room and headed down the corridor.

JAREK STUDIED THE WOMAN AND BOY from across the room. Sometime during the night, the satin duvet had been pushed to the bottom of the bed.

Sarah lay on her side, with her bad arm stretched across Rashid's stomach. His son lay in the curve of her belly, cuddled close with his head resting in the hollow of her shoulder.

Jarek forced the fury in him to calm before he approached the side of the bed. She might have saved his son, but that didn't give her the right to build up Rashid's hopes.

Gently, he picked up his son and carried him to the guards. "Take him to his room," he ordered softly. He handed Rashid to Bash, the older of the two guards. "You can tell me later how he got past the two of you."

Waking, Rashid blinked, then frowned. "Papa? What time is it?"

"Time for Bash to take you to your own room," Jarek whispered.

"You got my note." Rashid nodded sleepily. "Papa, do you think you can make Sarah stay?"

"Everyone has their place in this world, Rashid. Sarah's is not with us."

The words were harsh, harsher than he intended.

When Rashid said nothing, Jared tapped his son's nose. "Sarah will be here, tomorrow. And for the ball."

"Really?"

"Yes." Jarek's mouth twitched. "Right now, it is time for more sleep. Soon it will be morning. You have breakfast and your lessons. If I am not mistaken, Trizal will be looking for you when your tutor calls."

"Yes, Papa." Rashid leaned over and kissed Jarek's cheek. Something he hadn't done for a very long time. Emotion squeezed Jarek's chest.

"Take him back, then return," he ordered the guards. "Both of you."

"Yes, Your Majesty," Bash answered, lifting the boy high against his chest.

Jarek watched the guards take Rashid down the hallway for a moment before he stepped back into Sarah's room.

Not thinking about the wisdom of his decision, he crossed to her bed.

Suddenly, as if sensing him, her eyes fluttered open. "Jarek? What are you doing here?" She glanced to her right, obviously looking for his son.

"I came in to check on you and found Rashid in your bed." Jarek reached over to the bedside lamp and switched it on.

Light flooded the room. Sarah blinked. "Yes, he crawled in during the night." Sarah sank back into the pillows, relieved. "He had a nightmare about scorpions, I think. He wanted to see how I was."

"How did he get past your guards?"

"I have guards?" Sarah asked, then frowned. "Am I a prisoner still?"

"How did he get past the guards, Sarah?"

"I don't know," she lied, not wanting to get the boy in trouble again. "I was asleep. Sandra gave me some pain killers for my arm."

"I appreciate what you did for Rashid on the ledge." The reminder forced him to soften his attitude. "But Rashid is becoming too attached to you, Sarah. It can only make things difficult later."

"You mean when I leave."

"Yes. When you leave."

"Have you decided when that will be?"

Jarek hadn't decided. "Just stay away from him, Sarah."

"Or what?" Maybe it was the pain killers, or the lack of sleep. Or maybe she was just afraid of the power this man and his son were gaining over her heart.

The same heart that would break the moment she said goodbye to them.

"Or deal with me." Jarek turned on his heel and started for the door.

"Anytime you're ready," Sarah sniped. "I'm not the one who keeps handing out orders, then running away."

"Running?"

Slowly, Jarek swung back. The anger rippled over his body, reminding her of a sleek dark panther ready to pounce.

"Yes. From our hotel room in New York. Then yesterday, when you didn't turn up in Morocco."

Jarek raised his eyebrow.

"Rashid told me how he followed you into the desert. That you wanted to be alone before I arrived."

"And you assume I was running from you. That I'm afraid of you?"

She recognized the angry flash in his eyes. How could one not when it practically seared the carpet between them? But something drove her, something pushed her to taunt him. "Why else would you not want to deal with me? It isn't the job, or the fact that you don't trust me or even dislike me. I'm sure you've met many others over the years you don't trust and don't care for. But very few you are afraid of."

"Do you want to do this right now?" The silk was back in Jarek's tone. Smooth and sharp as ever. "Right here?"

"If this is what it takes. I've done interviews in stranger places."

"I'm not talking about our interview." The challenge was there, thrown down between them. A gauntlet he dared her to pick up.

"No, we're talking about a war. Between you and I." She tilted her head back. "The trouble is in a war nobody wins.

Everyone walks away bloody and—" she stopped, unwilling to go any further. Unwilling to be the only one wearing emotions on their sleeve.

"And," he snapped. "What?"

She unleashed the panther and struggled for footing—on a dangerous, slippery slope.

"Heartbroken. Damn you." She punched the pillow with her hand, then cried out in pain.

"Of all the—" Jarek let out a long, frustrated sigh.

"Don't," she bit out and cradled her injury to her chest. "Don't you dare feel sorry for me."

"Sorry?" He let out a string of obscenities. "Of all the emotions you raise in me, pity is not one of them."

He grasped her shoulders, bringing her forward. "When I saw you in the plane, the years fell away. You hadn't changed. You tempted me, the first time I saw you and every minute in between."

"And now?"

"Especially now," he stated, with an arrogance that almost softened her heart. Almost.

His lips trailed lightly over her shoulder, nibbled on her neck. "I keep telling myself if I give in to temptation, I'll be satisfied." His mouth skimmed her jaw, kissed her temple. "If I tasted you, the craving would leave."

She shivered against him, heard him groan.

"Say my name," Jarek demanded softly, his gaze meeting hers before drifting down to her mouth as it had in the cave. "You said it earlier in fear when the Al Asheera nearly caught us at the plane. Say it now."

His fingers slid over the nape of her neck, buried themselves deep into the thick, strands of hair. He tugged her closer. "Say my name. This time without the fear, Sarah."

Her mind shouted at her to make some pithy remark. Something cutting and defensive. But in the end, she was left no choice.

She spoke from the heart.

"Jarek." She breathed the name against his lips, taking in the taste of him. A cigar, sweet wine. Both heady enough to make her mind swirl, her chest flutter.

His mouth captured hers, his tongue quickly moving inside. He tasted, stroked and explored until she moaned from the onslaught. Until she was the one shuddering, and he was taking the pleasure.

"Again." His palm slipped over her chest, through the silk of her nightgown, sending jolts of desire quaking through her.

"Jarek."

Slowly he raised her wrist and kissed the inside just under the bandage. His mouth lingered over the pulse until it fluttered.

"Don't," she whispered. The soft caress hurt her heart more than any insult or harsh words. "Haven't you already gotten what you want?"

"I've been fighting what I want," Jarek murmured. "And I'm too tired to fight now."

Unable to stop, Sarah's arms slipped around his back, ignoring the wince of pain beneath her bandage.

Desperate for more heat, her fingers parted his shirt from his pants, flexing then curling into the hard, tight skin at the base of his spine, the ridges that scoured—

Sarah gasped, her fingers frozen over the scars that crisscrossed his back. "My God, Jarek. What happened?"

Jarek stiffened. "Nothing."

"You call those scars nothing?"

Slowly, he shifted out of her arms, then stood. "As you said before, it's just a mark. And I have many others."

His words frosted the air between them. Cold enough to make her shiver, her heart freeze. "How many scars did they leave inside you, Jarek?"

"Too many." His eyes swept over her, his features carefully controlled. "You asked earlier for me not to pity you. Do not make the mistake and assume that I want sympathy from you, Sarah."

He walked to the door and paused. "I asked you earlier to limit your time with my son. He is growing attached to you and I don't want to see him hurt when you leave. Do you understand?"

"Yes."

"Good."

Sarah waited for the door to shut, for the emptiness she felt inside to fill the room. "I think I finally do understand."

ANNA AL ASADI was born curious. A trait her husband, Quamar, considered a flaw. One that left him frustrated most days, but one he took pleasure in most nights.

It was the same curiosity that pushed her to see Quamar for the first time lying injured in a hospital room many years before, and the same curiosity that brought her to Sarah Kwong's room that afternoon.

Of course, the fact Quamar mentioned Jarek's past attraction to the female reporter didn't hurt, Anna mused as she knocked gently on the huge, oak doors.

There was nothing on earth she treasured more than family. Having lost a brother to an assassin years before, she understood how easily family could be hurt or taken away.

And Jarek was family.

When the door swung open, Anna held up the pile of clothes draped over her arm. "I'm Anna Al Asadi. My husband, Quamar, mentioned you're in need of a few things to wear."

"Why, yes," Sarah answered and stepped back. "Thank you."

Anna took in the soft, curtain of ebony hair that settled around a graceful neck, the exotic lines of her face, the laser-sharp green eyes. Intelligent. Feminine. Beautiful.

"Please, come in. And it's Sarah."

Gracious.

"Then you must call me Anna." Definitely, queen potential, she thought, hiding her pleasure behind a sunny smile.

Word spread quickly in Taer. Stories even quicker. The fact that the Taerians found out about Sarah Kwong's heroism, her devotion to their young prince, had already endeared her to many.

Anna walked over to the bed and laid the clothes across the bottom corner. "I hope you've been comfortable?"

"Yes," Sarah answered, then gestured around the room. "I'd be pretty hard to please, if I wasn't."

It was the best of the six guest suites and Anna's favorite. A classic with its high ceilings, its strong but simple lines. But what she liked the most was the touch of romance and elegance with an oversized fireplace, the deep burgundy drapes and Persian rugs.

Across from the fireplace was a small sitting area that contained a floral print, flanked by rose-colored Queen Anne chairs.

Lavender filled various vases, both bone china and crystal, making the air sweet and soothing.

And it was also the bedroom closest to Jarek's quarters. A fact Anna definitely found interesting.

"Thank you for letting me borrow some of your clothes." Sarah stroked the mixture of silk blouses and cotton dresses that lay across the duvet.

Anna laughed. She'd long ago accepted her curves, blond hair and baby blue eyes. But every once in a while, the wish to be exotic…

"These aren't mine. Jarek had these ordered for you and brought up from the city."

"Really?" Instead of pulling her hand away, Sarah fingered the fine silk blouses, the brushed cotton skirts. "How did he know my size?"

"From the camisole and pants, before I had them burned," Anna answered. "You seem surprised."

"I guess I am," Sarah admitted then stepped back from the bed. "I didn't expect him to take the time."

The hurt was there, just beneath the surface, hidden by the set of her chin, the arms hugging her body.

Anna had been prepared to like Sarah. The fact that Lara Mercer had nothing but good things to say about her friend, had endeared Anna immediately.

What she hadn't expected were the protective feelings that arose almost instantly. Or the fierce sense of loyalty.

Anna nearly tsked in disgust. Lord knew, Jarek had suffered over the past several years. But misery, did not need company in this case. And no matter how Sarah tried to disguise her emotions, the woman was definitely miserable.

"You saved Prince Rashid," Anna explained, hiding her thoughts behind a sympathetic smile. "I think providing you with clothes was the least we could do."

"Yes, Rashid. I'd forgotten…" Sarah looked at Anna. "How is he?"

"He's fine—"

A soft tap on the door interrupted Anna. "Come in."

A woman entered with a tray of tea and scones.

"Hello, Miss Anna. Miss Sarah."

"Sarah, this is Nashemia. She will be taking care of you during your stay."

Sarah placed the servant's age at forty. Her chestnut hair was coiffed smoothly in a bun at the base of her neck. The severe style emphasized her slender build, the heart shaped face and big, somber eyes.

Nashemia smiled at Sarah, revealing a pretty row of white teeth. "I thought you both would like some tea." She set the tray down on the coffee table in front of the fireplace.

"If you need anything, just ring." The servant nodded toward the cordless phone on a nearby desk, then turned toward Anna. "Shall I draw a bath for Miss Sarah before I put her clothes away?"

"No, not yet I think. Maybe in an hour or so." Anna inclined her head. "Thank you, Nashemia."

"You are welcome." The woman bowed slightly, then excused herself.

Anna sat down on the settee. Conscious of Sarah's injury, she pointed toward the refreshments. "May I?"

"Yes, please." Sarah took her seat on the chair across from Anna.

"You have a kind heart." Anna picked up the teapot and filled the two cups. "And you've impressed Rashid. He told me about the scorpion and how you saved him from falling. By the time he was done, the scorpion was the size of a tiger and had fangs as well."

"He wasn't exaggerating. I've never seen a bigger bug in my life." Sarah smothered a chuckle. "The whole experience gave me more than a few gray hairs."

"Don't feel bad. I'll let you in on a secret," Anna whispered, conspiratorially. She handed Sarah her tea. "Quamar's fear of bugs is the reason he has no hair."

Sarah chuckled, almost jostling her cup. The reaction spurred both women into laughter.

After a few moments, they calmed down enough to sip their tea.

"I think Ramon's death is the only reason why Jarek has not punished Rashid for riding Ping out into the desert," Anna said, sobering.

"I think he's learned his lesson," Sarah suggested, remembering the cliff. "He's a brave little boy."

"You understand him," Anna stated, then decided to go with her instincts. "And, I believe, have grown to love him."

"Yes," Sarah answered truthfully. "I think from the first moment he looked at me with those soulful eyes and that baby face."

Anna nodded, understanding. "Sarah, do you want me to notify your family about your injuries?"

"No. The worst is over," Sarah explained. "It would only add to an already growing list of worries for them."

"Because of your job?"

"Mostly," Sarah replied. "Both my parents and older sister lead a calm existence. Not that I suffered because of it. Both my parents are loving, supportive, well-educated. I had your typical all-American childhood. The white picket fence, the swing set and tree house. No hidden skeletons. No drama."

"And journalism offered you a chance to change that," Anna reasoned over the rim of her tea. "A little excitement, in an otherwise normal life?"

Surprised, Sarah had never considered that before. "Maybe."

"Are you up for dinner tonight?" Anna asked, changing the subject. "Or would you prefer to eat in your room?"

"No." She glanced around. "I think I'd like to get out and explore a little."

"That might be more difficult than you think." Anna finished her tea and placed the cup back on the tray. "You have two guards outside, ready to accompany you wherever you need to go."

"You're joking."

"No, I'm not."

"Guards?"

"Think of them as escorts," Anna suggested. "It might help."

"I thought he was just threatening me. I had no idea he would go through with it."

"Go through with what?"

"Keeping me prisoner."

Chapter Nine

Dressed in white cotton slacks and a matching sleeveless blouse, Sarah opened her bedroom door.

Two soldiers immediately straightened to attention.

"Hello, gentlemen."

The older of the two, a man in his early fifties, inclined his head. "Hello, Miss Kwong. My name is Bash."

"Hello, Bash."

Bash nodded to the younger man, one closer to Sarah's own age, next to him. "This is Ivan. We will be your escorts during your stay here in Taer."

"You mean you are my guards." She smiled at the young man, immediately liking his warm brown eyes. And the fact that he tried not to smile. "It's a pleasure to meet you, Ivan."

"Thank you, Mistress."

"I was hoping to take a walk through the garden," Sarah explained. "I've seen it from my balcony and it looks absolutely beautiful."

Bash pointed down the hallway. "The stairs are at the end of this corridor."

"I admired your work on that biochemical incident in Las Vegas a few years ago, Miss Kwong," Ivan admitted as they walked toward the main staircase.

"Thank you, Ivan."

Bash cleared his throat to catch the younger man's attention, then shook his head.

"I didn't mean your work on the biochemical. I meant I've seen your news broadcast." Ivan nearly stumbled on the stairs. "Many of them. If they are big enough news stories, that is…we get to see them here on television."

Sarah saw Bash roll his eyes. She cleared her throat to smother a small laugh.

"I appreciate that, Ivan. Thank you again," Sarah replied. "Hopefully, my story on your king will make the news over here, too."

"I think that would be wonderful," Ivan replied, his face beaming.

"As we all do." Quamar approached them at the bottom of the stairs. He gave the two guards a quick nod.

"Good day, Sarah." He leaned down and kissed her cheek, then offered his arm. "May I?"

"Certainly," Sarah responded as she placed her hand through the crook of his elbow and followed through the terrace door.

"I'm glad to see you up and about, Sarah."

"That makes two of us."

They strolled through the patio, down the stairs and out to the garden. Sarah and Quamar caught Jarek scowling from his office balcony.

"Jarek looks angry," she commented following Quamar's gaze. "Did I do something again, without realizing?"

"No." Quamar chuckled. "I imagine he is thinking about the Al Asheera. Normally, Jarek has many things on his mind but with the rise of the Al Asheera, he has put most everything else aside."

"Including my interview."

"It's quite possible. He hasn't made a decision on your meeting yet."

"Maybe as his personal advisor, you can help me with some preliminary information, Quamar."

"Such as?"

"You could give me more insight to the Al Asheera," Sarah suggested. "I know they are a renegade group. The news reports from years ago stated that they overran the palace and killed Jarek's wife, Saree, and your uncle, Hassan Al Asadi."

Quamar steered her down one of the main paths and into the courtyard. "That is correct. They also killed Hassan's son, Zahid."

"All before you and Jarek were able to overtake them," Sarah added. "You saved Anna, didn't you? And Rashid?"

"You have done your research."

They stopped at a nearby olive tree. The shade gave them a brief respite from the hot sun. Sarah leaned up against its trunk.

She'd traveled throughout the Middle Eastern world. Turkey, Jordan and many similar countries. But none moved her more than Taer.

From her position she could see most of the palace. It rose from the rolling plains of the Sahara, boasting long lines of archways and columns that stood stoic for hundreds of years against golden crested towers.

How much would the technology—the oil production— tarnish the luster of the country?

"What I've learned is documented, public knowledge. And it is all I could find out," Sarah acknowledged. "And I'm really good at finding out things. There are gaps. Huge gaps. But everywhere I turn, I hit wall after wall on the attempted rebellion. Why is that, Quamar?"

"Maybe there is not much to tell?"

"Or maybe there is something to hide," Sarah deduced. When Quamar didn't answer, she tried a different tactic. "Your king does not strike me as a pushover. Somehow, someone got the best of him in order to get that close to his family."

"Many of the guards had been bribed by the rebels."

"Who leads the Al Asheera?"

"We do not know at this time. Their previous leader was killed during the attempted coup five years ago."

"Who was that?"

"I cannot say."

"You cannot or will not?"

"I will not," Quamar admitted. "That is Jarek's decision to tell you."

"Why? Was this person important?"

"A traitor is a traitor. Who they were before that is insignificant."

"But it would explain how they got close to Jarek's family." Sarah thought for a moment. "He's concerned there is another traitor within your walls isn't he? And he suspects it is me. Although the fact that I'd risk my own life in a plane crash to kill him is crazy."

"Crazy is always a concern when you are dealing with terrorists," Quamar commented. "But I do not believe Jarek considers you a threat, Sarah. However, the tracking device he discovered in your purse has us both puzzled."

"Me, too," she confessed. "I couldn't even begin to pinpoint a possible moment someone slipped it into my purse."

"If that's the case and you had nothing to do with the tracking, you also could have been a target."

"Or more likely a decoy," she responded. "Targeting me to be killed serves no purpose."

Started, Quamar looked at her. "It is not you. It is what you represent. You are American."

"So is Anna."

"No. Anna is Al Asadi now."

Sarah smiled at the possessive tone. "I stand corrected."

"There are still many people in Taer opposed to our relationship with your country, Sarah," Quamar explained. "What has kept us in balance is the friendship between our king and your president. And the respect that our people hold for Jarek. If something happens, such as your death, President Mercer and my king would have a hard time keeping the balance. The outrage of your country would force us to defend ours."

"But I am just another journalist."

"You are also Lara MacAlister's friend. She is the daughter of the President. You've come here on the recommendation of the President."

"I didn't get this job because of Lara," Sarah defended once again.

"Whether you did or did not, is not important. What is important is the perception of friendship. That and the fact you have a reputation of being tough, but fair. If you are successful, it would put their public relations in a far better light. I think the risk is worth the reward." Quamar paused, letting his words sink in. "Your death would make a statement. Especially now. Once you saved Rashid, you became Taer's heroine. Now two nations would mourn your death."

"And if I were proved a traitor to your king?"

"Disastrous."

"The president told me this assignment would be difficult," she acknowledged. "But never dangerous."

"Would it have made a difference?"

"No." She came for more than a story. She came for answers. Private answers that only Jarek could give her. Diplomatic agreement or not.

"He isn't an emotional man, your king," Sarah noted, making sure she nodded in Jarek's direction so he knew they were talking about him. If he asked her later, it would be her opening for a personal conversation.

"When you are king, you are not allowed to be."

"Yet he blames himself for the death of his wife, doesn't he?" Sarah pushed.

"A personal question?"

"It is. But not for my exposé. Just for my curiosity."

"You will have to ask him," Quamar stated solemnly. He started them back toward the palace. "Only he can say what is in his heart."

"Oh, I will," she promised. "But first, I need to find out if he has a heart."

Chapter Ten

That night, Jarek surprised Sarah by meeting her at the bottom of the stairs for dinner. He'd shed the last two days in the desert easily enough. As a snake would its skin, she thought with more than a little resentment.

His trimly tailored, gray Armani suit was a far cry from the sweat-darkened shirt and dirt-stained riding pants. Grudgingly, she admitted, he wore them both well.

"Your Majesty," Sarah greeted him with a deep curtsy. A custom that struck her strange, considering the last few days.

"Miss Kwong." Jarek took her hand as she straightened and brought her fingers to his lips. "That must have been painful," he murmured.

"You have no idea," she responded, tugging her hand free.

"Is it your arm?" Anna asked, her brow knitted with concern. She wore a sapphire-blue dress that accented the short bob of blond hair and her baby blue eyes.

The dress's sweetheart neckline and snug fit showed off her feminine curves and shapely legs to perfection, making Sarah more than a little self-conscious over her somewhat boyish figure.

"Maybe you should have stayed in your bed one more day, Sarah," Anna suggested.

"I'm fine." Sarah smiled reassuringly, ignoring Jarek's raised eyebrow. "And dinner with you is just what the doctor ordered."

Quamar took Anna's elbow and led her through the dining room doors, while Jarek offered his arm to Sarah.

Reluctantly, she accepted, slipping her uninjured hand over his forearm. But the disdain was there, if only in the rigid nod of her head.

"Sarah, Ian MacAlister told me once that you were the last person he ever expected his wife, Lara, to be friends with," Anna commented, while the servants served the first course of shrimp almandine.

The dinner table had been set for the adults only. At first Sarah wondered if it was because of Jarek's order to keep distance between Rashid and her. But Ivan explained that normally Jarek, Quamar and Anna dined with the children earlier in the evening, whenever possible, to avoid conflict with bedtimes. Tonight the children dined in their quarters.

"Yes, I suppose he would say that." Sarah chuckled, not at all offended. It actually felt good to laugh, she had done very little in such a long time. "And honestly, I would have to agree with him. Lara gets the credit for our friendship."

"How so?" Jarek asked the question, but his face remained expressionless. Sarah couldn't decide if his interest was piqued or he was just being polite.

She wore a simple silk dress, the color of burgundy wine. The silk dipped and flowed from a haltered neckline to a slightly flared skirt at her hips. Her hair had been brushed and left in a long, straight curtain between bare shoulder blades. Like in the desert, she wore no earrings, only the jade pendant that now hung low between her breasts.

"I actually was a newspaper reporter at the time I met

Lara. We crossed paths in the public bathroom at one of the casinos on the Las Vegas strip. I recognized her instantly. Her father was the vice president under your father, President Cambridge, Anna. Lara had become somewhat of a celebrity during that time."

"And she didn't know you were a reporter?" Anna asked, obviously enjoying the story.

"No, she didn't. I wasn't quite as recognizable at the time."

"So then what happened?" Anna asked the question before biting into a buttered roll.

"I happened to be changing my niece's diaper at the time and struck up a conversation about children. At one point, she admitted to me she was pregnant. Of course, she didn't tell me who the father was, but rumors were already circulating about her and Ian MacAlister."

"And you reported it?" The disbelief in Anna's tone made Sarah laugh.

"Oh, yes. It made the headline news," Sarah explained. "The next time I saw her was the day after the story broke. I thought for sure she would punch me in the face."

"Did she?" It was Quamar who asked.

"No, but I think she was tempted if only for a second or two. After all, I had a microphone in her face at the time she realized I was a reporter."

"What did she do?" Jarek prompted, intrigued in spite of himself.

"She laughed and told me to look her up in a month for an exclusive interview." Sarah thought for a moment. "I think it was the only time in my life I'd ever been flabbergasted. From that moment, we were destined to be friends, I think."

"So did you follow up with her?"

"No, actually." Sarah placed her fork down on the table and wiped her fingers on her napkin.

"Later that day I found out about a biochemical terrorist plot to take down half the city of Las Vegas. I covered the story. That, combined with Lara's pregnancy, put me on track for national news. The rest is history."

"I was there," Quamar said quietly. "A government agent turned traitor. Lara was shot in the stomach by his son."

"Yes. But thankfully the baby wasn't harmed." Jarek noted that Sarah quit eating and instead rested her hands in her lap. He summarized that she didn't want to ruin dinner by drawing attention once again to her injury. She'd lost weight in the desert, at least five pounds in his estimate. She couldn't afford to lose more. He made a mental note to have some food sent up to her room later in the evening.

"I never reported that part of the events. It had become too personal at that point, I guess. I found myself visiting her while she recovered and we became friends."

"Lara affects many people that way, I think." Quamar winked.

Sarah grinned before turning to Anne. "She told me your families have grown closer over the years."

"Yes, with United States presidents for fathers, you tend to share similar life experiences," Anna replied easily enough.

Sarah understood that life hadn't been that easy for Anna Cambridge-Al Asadi. Several years before, Anna's younger brother and grandmother had been killed by an assassin during a plot to kill her father. Sarah knew that somehow the MacAlister family had played a role in helping Anna through the loss she'd suffered.

"I'm looking forward to seeing Lara and Ian's new baby when we visit in a few days," Anna exclaimed.

"Beau." Sarah smiled. "Beau Mercer MacAlister. He's adorable. And now that Clare is four, she is a terrific big sister."

Rashid rushed into the room. "I'd be a better big brother."

"Ready to say good-night?" Jarek asked, taking the safer route and ignoring Rashid's boast.

"Yes." But he surprised those in the room by going to Sarah first and giving her a kiss on the cheek.

"You will be here in the morning, right, Sarah?"

"Yes, Your Highness," she answered, then gave him a small squeeze for added reassurance.

Rashid hugged Jarek a moment later. "Good night, Papa."

"Good night, son."

Rashid jumped into Quamar's lap. "Good night, Uncle Quamar."

"Good night, Your Highness," Quamar said seriously, only to tickle the little boy a moment later. Rashid rolled off his uncle's lap in a peel of laughter.

Sarah laughed, hoping that it would be awhile before Rashid lost the playful innocence that came with childhood. At least in that, she had to commend Jarek. He had given his son a tremendous gift by allowing him to be a child.

Something she was sure he'd never had.

"Come on, sport." Anna took Rashid's hand. "It's time for me to put Kadan and Jenna to bed, too. You can help me with Jenna."

She paused to give Quamar a kiss. "I'll be back in a little while. Don't hold dessert on my account."

Quamar chuckled. "You are done being mad, then?"

"No. But we can work that out later. Alone," she promised, then gave him a slow sexy wink as she walked out of the room with Rashid.

"Mad?" Jarek asked, his frown deepening after watching the interchange between his son and Sarah.

Rashid's obvious affection for Sarah was proving to be a bigger problem than he had anticipated.

"Anna is not happy that we are going out to the plane crash site tomorrow," Quamar stated. "She believes the Al Asheera might use the opportunity to set a trap for us."

"You're going to the site to retrieve Ramon's body?" Sarah asked.

"We will try," Quamar responded slowly. "It has been three days since the accident. There will be little left of our friend, but we will bring back what we can."

"I also want to see if there is any evidence of foul play on Ramon's part," Jarek answered. "It might help clear up the matter of the tracking device."

"I'd like to go," Sarah stated. "And before you tell me no, Your Majesty, I would like to point out that this directly affects me."

"No," Jarek replied, dismissing her argument. "You are still recovering from your injury."

She glanced at her bandage. "The swelling is almost gone and so is the pain. I'm more than capable of going with you."

Quamar noticed the hesitancy on Jarek's part. He also noticed the tension between the couple. Quamar knew his cousin and knew he was struggling for indifference.

"Ramon's death is not part of your news, Miss Kwong."

"I agree, Your Majesty. But this is not only about Ramon, it is about the Al Asheera," Sarah said, firmly.

"They are an issue for my country to deal with," Jarek answered, but his tone was low, just short of harsh. "The Al Asheera do not need media attention for their treachery."

"I will not mention them specifically. But I think their involvement will only add public opinion to your commitment to this partnership with America."

"I think that would be a good idea, Your Majesty," Quamar stated. "I have enough men. With Bash and Ivan she would be well-protected. And guarded," he added with a twitch to his lips.

Jarek looked at his cousin, his eyes narrowed in suspicion. He understood his cousin well enough to know that something motivated Quamar's suggestion. He just didn't know what.

Finally, Jarek nodded, his royalty showing in that one short movement. "All right. I will agree against my better judgment. But you had better follow orders. My orders."

EARLY THE NEXT MORNING, Bash and Ivan escorted Sarah to the courtyard where Quamar and Jarek waited.

Like her, both men were dressed in khaki pants and light linen shirts. A set of clothes, she noted, that matched most of the men around her. A uniform of sorts for the desert.

It took them less than an hour to reach the plane by jeep.

Quamar ordered a team of eight soldiers ahead to check out the wreckage.

"Bash, go with King Jarek." Quamar jumped out of their jeep and followed the men.

"Ivan, stay with Miss Kwong," Jarek commanded. "And remember my orders."

Bash shot Ivan a stern look and followed Jarek across the sand.

"What did the king mean? Remember my orders?"

"You're to be kept at a thirty-meter distance, Miss Sarah."

"A hundred feet. Why?"

"The king must announce the site safe," Ivan advised. "Then you'll be able to join the others."

"Why did Bash frown at you, Ivan?"

Ivan smiled. "He was warning me to be on my best behavior and to perform my duty. He said I was too exuberant in my conversation with you the other night." Ivan blushed. "I do apologize, Miss Kwong. I sometimes get carried away."

Sarah's lips twitched with humor. "There is no need to apologize—"

Suddenly, Quamar shouted Jarek's name in warning. Sarah swung around just as explosion hit the air.

Ivan threw himself on Sarah, covering her with his body.

"Jarek!" Sarah gasped his name, fear hit her full force. Without realizing it, Sarah screamed and shoved Ivan off of her.

"Jarek," she whispered. Another explosion hit near the plane. Fear grabbed at her, clenching her gut while she searched the mayhem of men running in different directions.

Suddenly, Jarek tackled Bash a few yards away. It took a moment to realize that the older soldier's clothes were on fire. Jarek rolled around with Bash, using the sand to smother the flames.

She was grasped by the arm. "Stay here," Ivan instructed, swearing.

Quamar ordered two soldiers over to the plane where two men lay unmoving on the ground. Sarah could tell from the blood and broken bodies that both men were dead.

"We need a medic over here!" Jarek yelled the command.

Ignoring Ivan's order, Sarah raced to Bash's side. Sand and blood covered the raw burns on his face and arms. Black soot covered his clothes and the rancid scent of smoke and burnt flesh filled the air.

Bash looked up at her, his light brown eyes hazy with pain. He could do little more than gasp for breath.

"Jarek," Sarah yelled. "Bash needs something to help him breathe."

"I have it." Quamar dropped beside Sarah and placed an oxygen mask over the soldier's mouth. "Bash, the helicopter is on its way. It will be here in a few moments."

Jarek grabbed Sarah's arm and pulled her to her feet. "I want you back in the jeep."

"No."

Jarek shook her sharply. "Listen to me. There could be other mines set around here."

"I'm staying with him." Sarah's words came out numb and hoarse. "At least until the helicopter gets here. Please?" Her gaze found Jarek's through blurred tears. "He wouldn't have been hurt if I hadn't insisted on coming."

"I will stay with her, Your Majesty," Ivan stated solemnly from behind her. "And Bash. I promise no harm will come to either of them."

"I don't want anymore—" Jarek stopped when he noticed the look on the younger man's face. "All right. Damn it. But watch her well. Do you understand me, Ivan?"

"Yes, Your Majesty."

Jarek turned to Quamar, who remained near Bash's side. "How did you know?"

Quamar pointed to the dead bird lying only a few yards away. "When was the last time you have seen a vulture killed by a bullet?"

Swearing, Jarek leaned down and pulled what looked like a piece of hair from around Bash's ankle. "Quamar." He handed it to his cousin.

"This wire is thread thin. A new technique that only an

expert would have access to," Quamar observed, twining the wire around his forefinger. "A specialist did this. Not the Al Asheera. They have no one with this expertise."

Anger whipped through Jarek's features, cold fury that chilled his blood. "So they are recruiting from the outside. For that they need money."

"A neighboring country?"

"Or a private venture," Jarek added. "Both would want control of the oil. Both could afford backing the Al Asheera."

"Jarek," Quamar said, his voice only low enough for his cousin to hear. "The bottom line is that someone knew you were coming to the site."

"As we suspected. Which is why I didn't want Sarah here in the first place," Jarek acknowledged, his tone sharp with anger. "The question is how did they know."

Quamar scanned the men now fighting to put out the fire. "Or who?"

Chapter Eleven

Sarah stepped into the king's outer office just as a pendulum clock chimed, marking the top of the four o'clock hour.

The man's eyes sharpened behind wire-rimmed glasses. He pulled his pocket watch from his suit vest and checked the time.

She sensed irritation shifting through him. He was a tall man, thin with a slight stoop that had become more noticeable in his later years. His features were hawkish in nature. Mostly because of a severely hooked nose than from the long, boney features and the ring of gray around a rather pointed head.

From what she knew about him, after twenty-five years serving the royal family of Taer, few things tended to annoy him. Reporters were one of them. Lack of manners and lack of respect for his country and its traditions were others.

She supposed that in his eyes, she seemed to represent all three.

"Hello, Miss Kwong." His voice was even, with no hint of his displeasure underlining the tone. "I am Trizal Lamente, His Majesty's personal secretary."

"Hello, Mr. Lamente." Sarah reached to shake hands, only to bite back her own impatience when Trizal refused to acknowledge the gesture. She let her hand drop to her side. "I received a call a few minutes ago. I believe His Majesty is expecting me?"

For the past few hours, she'd paced her room, unable to get permission to see or information regarding Bash.

Anna was out on a scheduled charity committee meeting and Quamar had been holed up with Jarek all afternoon.

Finally a call had come through less than fifteen minutes before by one of Lamente's assistants, advising Jarek would see Sarah at four o'clock.

"Yes, he is expecting you," Trizal confirmed. "Follow me, please."

"Thank you."

Sarah's heels tapped lightly on the marble tiled floors of the corridor. She'd worn a new navy blue suit for the meeting. One that Jarek provided. Cut stylish enough to be feminine, but conservative enough to show her professionalism.

They stopped at the end of the hallway in front of a set of mahogany double doors. Lamente gave a short, rather efficient knock.

"Come in."

The secretary opened the door and gestured Sarah in before him. "Your Majesty, Miss Kwong."

"Thank you, Trizal."

The secretary bowed, then shut the door with a firm snap.

"Your Majesty." Sarah offered a small curtsy. "I don't think your secretary approves of me."

"Don't take it personally, Sarah." Jarek stood and came

around from his desk. "Most times he doesn't approve of me, either."

"Nor does he like me." Quamar grinned. "I am too barbaric."

"Hello, Quamar."

"Sarah." Quamar gave her a big hug. "How are you holding up?"

"Better than Ivan, I think," she said, referring to the young guard she had left standing outside the offices.

"We would have called you before this, but Bash has been in surgery since he arrived at the hospital," Jarek stated. "He is now in recovery. The doctor said he did well, considering."

"When can I see him?"

It was Quamar who answered. "I am going to see Bash now that I'm finished here. I will take you with me, if you'd like."

"Yes, very much so."

Jarek leaned back against his desk and crossed his arms. "Sarah, I must warn you not to use Bash's accident in your exposé."

Sarah jerked as if she'd been slapped. "I'm sorry, could you repeat that?"

"I cannot allow you to use Bash's misfortune as part of your article."

"Let me get this straight." Sarah articulated each word slowly, trying to hold on to her temper. "You think I'm going to exploit Bash?"

"Not necessarily. However, I wanted to make sure we understood each other."

"I understand you perfectly," Sarah acknowledged with disdain. "It seems to me you're the one who doesn't understand, Your Majesty."

Quamar hid a smile behind a dry cough. "I do not think an interview was your intention, was it, Sarah?"

"No," Sarah answered tightly. "It wasn't."

"Whether I thought it was or not, I still needed to be clear," Jarek reiterated. "I will not have any of my people publicly humiliated."

"I think you've made yourself crystal clear. No questions from the reporter," she answered, annoyed. "May I see Bash now?"

Jarek stared at her for a long second. His jaw tightened but he said nothing until he walked back around to his desk. "Quamar, will you please escort Miss Kwong to the infirmary." He dismissed her by taking up a few papers and hitting the intercom button on his desk. "Trizal, Miss Kwong is leaving. I need you to come in here for a moment."

"Yes, sir."

"Thank you, Your Majesty." Sarah took the dismissal for what it was. She curtsied, rather stiffly, then turned on her heel and walked toward the door in quick, angry strides.

"Miss Kwong," Jarek called out, stopping her midstride. "One more thing."

She faced him, her spine rigid. "Yes?"

"If you would, please give Bash my regards and tell him I will be by later to see him."

"Later?" Sarah nearly snorted. What could be more important than seeing to the well-being of one of his soldiers?

As if he heard her, Jarek added, "Two other of my soldiers died at the crash site today. Soldiers who had wives, children and parents. I need to speak with the families, let them know of the attack and offer my condolences. It is the priority."

Startled, Sarah found herself turning back toward Jarek.

For the first time, she noticed the pain in the darkest part of his black eyes.

Once again, Jarek surprised her. How can a man be so insensitive one moment, then so compassionate the next? Suddenly, Sarah realized how. Jarek risked being insensitive to her in order to protect Bash. One of his people. Just as he'd said.

"I'll give Bash your message."

A long silence settled between them, until Quamar discreetly cleared his throat.

"One more thing," Jarek added, his voice now huskier. "Your personal things were destroyed in the fire today."

"It doesn't matter. I have enough to get me through."

"You're going to need clothes for tomorrow. We're going to the oil field. We need to increase the security there and I'm assuming you would like to take a look around."

"Yes, I would like to go with you." Sarah hesitated, unsure of where the offer came from. "It will give me an opportunity to report on the progress of the oil drilling."

"That was my thought as well. We leave first thing in the morning," Jarek ordered. "I'll make sure there are clothes for you in the morning."

"All right. Thank you."

Trizal opened the door.

"Are you ready, Sarah?" Quamar asked gently.

"Yes."

Quamar walked with her outside, leaving Ivan to follow a few steps behind.

"I didn't realize that this would affect him, too," Sarah murmured. "I should have."

"Jarek takes loss, any kind of loss, personally," Quamar answered solemnly. "It is what a king does, if he is a good king. And believe it or not, Sarah, Jarek is an excellent king."

SARAH STEPPED OFF the hospital elevator. Antiseptic thickened the air in the corridor, stinging her nose and eyes. They headed down to the hallway to Bash's room.

"Here." Quamar stopped at the third door.

Before they entered, Nashemia stepped out.

Startled, the servant looked up. "I'm sorry, mistress. I didn't see you."

"It's all right," Sarah answered softly. "Are you a friend of Bash's?"

"Yes," she said. "He was very kind to me when I first arrived here."

"How is he?" Quamar asked.

"Resting, Master Al Asadi." Nashemia's eyes teared. "Dr. Haddad says that he suffered burns on his chest, back and arms. But that he is lucky."

"Do not worry, Nashemia." A man walked up behind the trio, his white hair short and stark against otherwise tanned features. "He will be fine. His recovery will be a long and arduous one, but he will recover and that's the most important thing."

"Yes," Nashemia answered, bobbing her head. "If you all will excuse me, I must get back to the palace."

"Of course," Quamar replied. "I'm sure Miss Kwong will keep you informed."

"Thank you," she said and hurried down the hallway.

Quamar clasped the doctor on his shoulder. "Sarah, may I introduce you to our royal physician? Dr. Omar Haddad."

"It is nice to meet you, Miss Kwong," he said, and shook Sarah's hand.

"Thank you, Dr. Haddad." She smiled, liking the older man immediately. "Are you Dr. Sandra Haddad's father?"

"Yes."

"She treated my injury the other day," Sarah commented, seeing the same shape of eyes, the small cleft in the chin that Sandra had inherited. "Of course, her reputation is worldwide. You must be very proud of her work in advanced synthetic viruses."

"I am." Pride flitted across the older man's features. "She has been a blessing to her mother and I."

"Actually," Quamar corrected. "Sandra needed a break from her research and is now our temporary coroner."

Dr. Haddad snorted. "Her break has been for over two years now. She is not temporary."

Sarah sensed the underlining disapproval from the older gentleman but didn't comment.

"How bad are Bash's injuries, Doctor?" Quamar asked, changing the subject.

"Over fifteen percent of his chest, arms and back are burned. He's very lucky that King Jarek got to him as soon as he did. His burns could have been much worse. If we can stop any infection, he should grow back a third of his skin and we'll graft the remaining. The king has already made arrangements for a team of specialists to fly in over the next few days to take a look at Bash."

"He did?"

"Yes. King Jarek is very concerned," Dr. Haddad responded, slowly, obviously curious over Sarah's response. "We've been keeping him up to date on an hourly basis."

Surprised, Sarah didn't comment. "Would it be possible to talk to Bash, Doctor?"

"Only for a few minutes. He has just been given a sedative for the pain and will need rest. Within the next few hours, we'll be moving him to a sterile room so we can remove his bandages. It's being prepared now."

Sarah nodded and stepped into the room. Bash lay

against the white sheets, a bandage covered his arms and chest. Another wrapped his forehead.

"Bash?"

The guard turned toward her, his eyes dull from the drugs.

"Miss Kwong?" Automatically he tried to sit up using his hand for leverage. He let out a small grunt of pain and fell back against the pillows.

"Please lie still, Bash. No need to cause yourself discomfort," she told him. "Is there anything I can do for you? Anyone you need me to notify?"

"No. The pain is minimal," he lied. His face appeared paler than the sheets behind him; his voice no more than a thin whisper.

"The king is arranging for your family to fly in from Europe, Bash." Quamar explained quietly. "They should be here the day after tomorrow. King Jarek will come later today."

"Thank you, sir."

"See you tomorrow then, okay?"

"There is no need."

"There is for me." Sarah's smile wobbled and the tears gathered behind her eyes. "You are my friend, Bash."

"Thank you, Miss Sarah."

Quamar nodded to Ivan, a silent signal for the younger man to stay a moment longer. When Quamar and Sarah stepped out of the room, she noticed that Bash's eyes had already closed.

"That was very kind of you," Quamar noted. "Most people wouldn't have come and visited a soldier."

"Not kind," she admitted. "If I hadn't insisted on going to the crash site, he wouldn't have been injured."

"Bash knows the risks that come with his job, Sarah. Do not blame yourself."

"I'm glad his family is coming." She thought of her family. No matter how different their paths have gone, she would be nothing without their support and love.

"Trizal is completing the arrangements."

A thought suddenly occurred to Sarah. "Quamar, did Ramon have any family?"

"He has a daughter living in London," Quamar answered. "Trizal has not yet been able to contact her. Once he does, Jarek will arrange for her flight to Taer."

"Were Ramon and the king close?" Sarah asked.

"They had grown closer over the past few years," Quamar answered quietly. "Ramon was the much younger brother of an old friend. Now they are both dead."

"Both?"

"Arimand was Jarek's Captain of the Guards. During the rebellion, the Al Asheera left him hanging in a tree for the buzzards," Quamar said grimly. "He died in my arms."

"Where was Jarek?"

"He was in a cell beneath the palace. Being tortured by the Al Asheera."

Chapter Twelve

For the second time in three days, Sarah flew over the Sahara in a royal plane.

"The fields are to the northeast of the country. An hour by airplane. Nearly a day by car. Half that by train."

Over the crest of the horizon rose two towers. The steel beams crisscrossed up three stories, ending in a narrow point that flashed bright like a beacon in the sunlight.

"Land rigs." Jarek pointed to the nearest tower outside of the window. "Most of the equipment and materials you see were provided by the United States after we made our tentative agreement to do business with them. Now that we've started production, they receive the majority of our crude oil. In return, they give us money and access to certain technology your government is developing."

"Is that why you chose not to join OPEC?"

"The oil market is changing. We have other industries like textiles to help sustain Taer. We are using the oil as a bargaining chip for more sophisticated technology. We want to be with the United States in the forefront of new energy technology. This is the first step. We could not do that with ties to OPEC. Already we are seeing a surge in our population. Some from foreigners, but others who are returning to our country—educated professionals—because we are now productive and can offer them competitive jobs."

"What kind of technology did we agree to share with you?"

"Alternative fuel and energy. Wind and solar, mostly, with some communication technology. Also Nano and others."

"Weapons?" She studied the soldiers patrolling the perimeter. Others stood guard over several buildings and the land rigs.

"Some," he acknowledged slowly.

"Like the Apache helicopters that flew us in from the desert?"

"Yes. While most of our neighboring countries approve of our agreement with the Americans, others are not so…open to our relations overseas. It leaves us vulnerable."

"People who don't appreciate social advancement?"

"Essentially, yes. Many believe in the old ways. Others believe we should show unity only to our own people."

"And what do you believe?"

"I believe in unity and tradition. But I also believe in progress. My position is to find a balance for all three."

"Any one of those other countries could be behind the Al Asheera's attack on the plane?"

"Yes. In theory." Jarek studied the oil site below. "I do not know for sure. But I've been trying to find out through different channels. So far, I have discovered nothing to support my suspicions."

One of the guards in the front seat handed Jarek two yellow hard hats.

"You'll need to put this on." Jarek gave her a hat.

"How long will it take for you to get the oil fields fully operational?"

"We are relying heavily right now on the United States for its training and specialists. The man in charge of the transition is Booker McKnight. He's an American. One of the last working here. Most of the others have left over the last several months. I've arranged for him to give you a tour while I take care of some business."

They landed on a single strip runaway of packed dirt and immediately loaded into two black SUVs with four soldiers. Quamar in the first. Sarah and Jarek in the second.

Sarah expected a little village filled with people. What she found beside the two steel land rigs were several huge white oil containers and a line of single barracks. Twenty single rooms that looked more like small storage units. Each held little more than two single beds, a toilet and lockers. A pair of mobile trailers were parked toward the end. One for mess and one for the site manager's office.

Bulldozers, excavators and cranes spotted the area. "Do they use the machines for landfills and trenching?" she asked Jarek.

But it wasn't Jarek who answered.

"Yes, and adding roads or airstrips."

The man was dressed in jeans and T-shirt. He wore a New York Yankees baseball cap with a handkerchief tucked into the back to protect his neck. He was a big man, tall, with heavyweight muscles that stretched a dull, gray T-shirt tight across a massive chest and tucked into a low-riding pair of Levi's jeans.

A pair of sky-blue eyes flickered over her with absolute male appreciation. For once, Sarah was glad she was wearing big framed sunglasses. It wasn't too often she was taken by surprise.

"Miss Kwong," Jarek introduced. "My field foreman, Booker McKnight."

"A pleasure to meet you," Booker said, a smile widened across his sun-darkened features. "A real pleasure."

Because she felt Jarek stiffen behind her, she sweetened her own smile. "Likewise," she replied, then realized she truly meant it. "You said airstrips. There is more than one?"

"We have three," Booker responded. "The one you landed on is for private planes. There are two other, larger strips we use for cargo."

Booker turned to Jarek. "I'm sorry to hear about Ramon, Your Majesty."

Jarek gave a short nod. Sarah noticed his jaw tightened, a dead giveaway to the depth of the king's feelings.

"You knew Ramon?" she asked, for no other reason than to draw Booker's attention from Jarek and give the king a second to wrestle down his emotion.

"When Ramon wasn't needed at the palace, he would make personnel runs for us. Give the men a chance to see their families," Booker acknowledged. "I don't have family here, but most of my men appreciated the opportunity."

"Before Ramon died, he mentioned a man by the name of Roldo. You wouldn't happen to know if he was a friend of Ramon's, would you?" Sarah asked, her instincts suddenly alert.

Booker's gaze flickered to Jarek's before he answered. "We have a demolition guy who works for us occasionally. His name is Roldo Costa."

"Demolition? As in explosives?"

"Yes. Sometimes we have to blast some of the site. Al Qassar shipping keeps explosive experts on retainer. We use their men since we have a contract with the company," Booker answered slowly.

"And Roldo is one of those experts," she prompted.

"Sarah, you are out here to get information on the drilling site. Not to investigate a murder," Jarek demanded.

"My apologies," Sarah replied, but her eyes narrowed into slits of green ice. Hungry for answers, she wasn't about to let this bone go. "I caught Booker's look, Your Majesty. Obviously, you knew that Roldo worked for Al Qassar."

"Yes, Quamar discussed the situation with Booker yesterday." Jarek let out a long sigh. "But that has nothing to do with you or your story. Booker has agreed to take you on a tour, while Quamar and I take care of some business. You will be safe with him."

"Fine." Sarah planted a wide smile on her face. "So, Mr. McKnight—"

"Booker will do," he said, trying to cover a grin.

"All right, Booker," she responded, turning on the charm. "I have to admit, I don't think I've had a better looking babysitter."

"Sarah," Jarek warned.

"I'm sorry, Your Majesty." She nearly batted her eyes. "Don't let me keep you from your business."

"Do not step out of line," Jarek warned before he turned on his heel. Two Royal Guards fell into step with their king.

Sarah's eyes lingered on him until he reached the main office.

"I guess I won't let that 'good-looking' comment go to my head," Booker murmured.

"I'm sorry. Sometime my temper gets away from me."

"No, problem. Ma'am." He tilted his cap back farther on his head. "Ready for the grand tour, Miss Kwong?"

"It's Sarah. And yes, I'm ready." She reached into her bag and pulled out her recorder.

She punched the record button. "Now tell me, how many people are you in charge of here?"

"We have almost thirty men. Including the cooks," Booker continued after a moment. "Each works twelve-hour shifts. Six days a week."

"That's a lot of hours."

"They like the money," Booker replied, studying the recorder. He tapped the dent with his finger. "Looks like your equipment got banged up a bit."

"A bullet winged my purse. Destroyed my wallet but only nicked the recorder."

"A bullet?"

"Long story. One you can ask your boss about later." Sarah smiled at Booker's confused expression. "Does everyone here work on the rig?"

"Most do." He gestured to the train tracks a few hundred yards in the distance. "Some are handlers. They load the crude oil onto the tanker train."

"Train?"

"We ship the crude oil to the ports by tanker train." He pointed to south of the drill site. "The tracks go directly through Taer and then travel farther south to the Qassar shipping yards. Where they're loaded on ships."

"Qassar shipping," Sarah commented.

"Yes."

Sarah put her hand above her eyes to shield the glare of the sun. "And in the opposite direction? Where do the tracks lead?"

"Nowhere in particular. Sometimes the trains can be over two miles long, so we installed tracks for another ten miles. At the end is just a barricade made of cement and steel. A dead end, you might say."

Chapter Thirteen

The heat of the afternoon dissipated as the sun melted into the blurred line between sand and sky.

Anna lifted her baby girl up in the air and laughed when the child squealed. A boy, no more than four years old, played in the wade pool with Rashid.

"I hope I'm not interrupting," Sarah said softly. Although a few features separated both boys, they were both dark, like their fathers and could pass as brothers.

"Not at all." Anna smiled and set the little girl down. "I had a break in my afternoon schedule, so we decided to play a bit."

Rashid lifted his head from under the water. "Sarah! Are you here to swim?"

"I don't think so, sport. Not today." She brushed the wet hair from his forehead, watched the water spike his long sooty lashes. Her heart flopped in her chest. "Missed you today." Damning herself when she realized she spoke the words out loud.

"Me, too," he whispered back.

"I'm Kadan."

Grateful for the distraction, she turned to the younger boy and smiled. "Hello, Master Kadan."

"Guess how old I am."

"All right." Sarah knelt down next to him, took a moment to study him seriously, trying desperately not to laugh as the little boy puffed up his chest. "I think you're six years old."

Rashid rolled his eyes, but said nothing.

A smile flashed across Kadan's cherub face. "I'm almost five years old."

"Really?"

"No." Rashid took Sarah in with one somber glance. "He just turned four last month."

The baby squealed and slammed her hands into the water, splashing them all.

"And this is Jenna." Anna laughed at the baby she held steady in the foot-high water. Jenna jumped up and down on her tip toes.

"She's only a year," Kadan explained, with a small frown for his sister. "She doesn't even talk yet."

"Then I will forgive her for splashing me."

When the children turned back to the water, Anna patted the cement next to her. "Do you have a few minutes to fill me in on the site?"

Sarah glanced at Ivan who was standing a discreet distance away. "Yes, but only a few if that's all right. Ivan and I wanted to see Bash before I have to get ready for the ball tonight."

Anna nodded. "Quamar told me earlier that Dr. Haddad is pleased with Bash's progress."

"That's very good news."

Sarah took off her shoes and rolled up her pant legs. She sat down and put her feet into the cool water. She sighed and wiggled her toes for good measure. "That's heaven."

"It is, isn't it?" Anna chuckled. "Especially after a hot day out in the sand."

"And it was hot," Sarah admitted. "But exciting. I think I really could grow to love this country, Anna."

"I felt the same way when I first came out here. There is something calming in the colors, the endless sea of sand and textures."

"But recklessly wild, too," Sarah added.

"Exactly," Anna agreed. "Once, Quamar compared the Sahara to a woman. A beautiful woman, who refused to conform or be tamed."

"I can see that. Men certainly are fascinated by her, aren't they?"

"Yes. I believe so."

"I met one of those men today, I think," Sarah mused. "A man by the name of Booker McKnight."

Anna dipped the baby in the water. "The foreman at the drill site."

"Yes. What do you know about him?"

"Off the record?" Anna asked, but didn't take her eyes off of Jenna.

"Absolutely."

"I only have met him once," Anna confessed. Jenna tugged free of her mother and slapped at the water, then laughed when it splashed back at her.

"Booker arrived about six months ago. He stayed here at the palace one night. Spent most of the next day in conference with Jarek and Quamar, then he left for the site."

"Who did he replace?" Jenna wobbled, then latched onto Sarah's knee. She gripped the pants tight in her little fist.

"I don't remember the man's name, but he was French. He left shortly before Booker McKnight arrived. A family hardship, I think. Why?"

"Just reporter's instinct," Sarah answered, then dribbled some water down Jenna's shoulder and smiled when the baby squealed. "I caught a glance between him and Jarek. I just have a feeling he's holding a few secrets."

"He's from the States and is friendly enough. He speaks about five different languages and seems to know his job."

"I might be overanalyzing things."

"With everything that's happened in the last forty-eight hours, who could blame you?" Anna insisted.

"My life certainly has changed, hasn't it?"

Suddenly, water caught her right in the face, causing her to gasp.

Rashid laughed, a belly laugh that cut short on a gasp when Sarah splashed him back.

Within moments, Kadan had joined the fun and all three were drenched in water. Anna sat away with Jenna and they both clapped with delight over the fun.

"Pardon my interruption, madame. But it is time for his Highness's lessons."

"Master Trizal Lamente, may I introduce you to Miss Sarah Kwong." Gone was the warmth of Anna's tone. It was replaced by a gracious if somewhat bland introduction.

"We have already met." The older man bowed his head slightly. "Good afternoon, mademoiselle."

She inclined her head. "Monsieur Lamente."

"I did not realize you were spending time with the young prince. Perhaps I can arrange for his lessons—"

"That is not possible, Trizal. Please take Rashid for his studies." Jarek approached in quick, angry strides.

"Goodbye, Sarah," Rashid said sadly.

"Bye, Your Highness." Sarah kept her smile in place as to not upset Rashid. She was unwilling to let the young boy see the rage brewing in his father's eyes. She had grown to recognize the emotion in Jarek over the last several days.

Trizal glanced at Jarek, who dismissed him with a wave of his hand.

Slowly, Sarah stood, feeling much better facing him at her full height. Even if it only took her to his shoulder.

Jarek's eyes flickered over Sarah, taking in the wet blouse, and even wetter pants.

"The agreement was…" Jarek's voice held no emotion once the teacher and pupil disappeared onto the terrace "…you would have no contact with my family, Miss Kwong. You cannot tell me this meeting was unavoidable."

"That's exactly what I'm going to tell you," Sarah managed. "My breech wasn't on purpose. I was on my way to see Bash. I didn't notice the boys until it was too late. And I wasn't going to be rude to Anna."

"Why don't I believe you?"

"I don't know, Your Majesty. Maybe you judge everyone based on your own prejudices rather than on the facts?"

Anna's soft gasp echoed from behind Sarah. But she refused to take back her words. Only the tightening of Jarek's jaw showed she'd scored a direct hit.

"May we speak in private?" Although he addressed her with a question, she understood it was an order.

"Of course."

Deliberately, he reached down and grabbed a towel from a nearby chair and tossed it to her. "You might want to dry off before you give the servants an eyeful."

Sarah looked down and barely suppressed her gasp. The water had turned her shirt translucent enough to the see her breasts through her bra.

She held the towel up and turned to Anna. "Thank you for the fun."

"Oh, I think the fun is just about to begin." Anna's lips twitched with amusement. "But its been my pleasure."

Sarah waited for Jarek to go ahead a few steps before glancing back at Anna. "Could you do me a favor?"

"Sure."

"If I don't appear again after an hour or so. Could you have my personal belongings sent back to the States?"

Anna laughed outright. "I don't think it will be necessary. But if you don't want to be escorting your stuff back yourself, you might want to try and be a bit more reserved."

Sarah raised her eyebrow. "I've tried. It doesn't work."

THE STONY SILENCE didn't dissipate until they were back in Jarek's office.

"I agreed to have you here in my country only if you agreed to follow certain rules." Anger infused every word, every syllable. "Rules I reiterated last night in your room."

"It wasn't preplanned, Your Majesty," she repeated. Sarah understood she was in the wrong, but it didn't stop her from stating her defense. "I saw Anna and stopped. I didn't see the children playing in the wade pool until it was too late."

"You didn't hear them splashing? Them laughing?"

His anger fed her own. "I heard splashing. But I won't be rude to a child. No matter who his father is," she said sharply and tossed the towel on the table.

If he didn't like that, too bad.

"Let me make myself understood, Miss Kwong." The words were grounded through his teeth, his eyes locked on her face. "You will not instigate any contact with my son. Are we clear? Because if it happens again, it will be the last thing you will do in my country."

"Throw me out, then." Anger seized Sarah with two

fists. Damn it, she wanted things out on the table. "Since the plane, you've run hot and cold. One moment you don't like me, then next you want to make love to me. Either way you have barely managed to be civil. You've threatened to imprison me, then threatened to toss me out on my ear. Make up your mind."

"How can I?" He grabbed her by the shoulders and drew her up until their noses almost touched. "When I'm damn sure I've lost my mind."

Swearing, his mouth settled over hers.

She expected anger and frustration.

His lips caressed hers, coaxing, tasting, shaping them beneath his mouth.

Instead, he gave her tenderness…pleasure…seduction.

The world stopped around them. No intrusions, no demands—except for the ones their own desire made.

He gathered her close, fitting her body to his even as his kiss continued until she surrendered on a sweet shudder and sigh.

With a growl, he deepened the kiss, his tongue no longer coaxing but demanding a response.

Her arms slipped around his back, gripping him tighter as she arched against his body.

When that wasn't enough, her fingers tugged in frustration, loosening his shirt from his waistband. This time when her hand skimmed his back, he didn't pull away. She felt the ridges, the deep scars that crisscrossed his back and whimpered at the pain he must have endured.

"Don't," he murmured and kissed her again, driving her thoughts away from his demons.

Without warning, glass shattered behind Sarah. Jarek swore and shoved her to the ground.

"Stay down."

His body was hard against hers, comforting for a brief moment before he rolled off her and onto his knees.

Blood, warm and sticky spread through her blouse. It took her a moment to realize it was his blood.

"Jarek!" A freight train of fear slammed into her. Before she recovered her balance, she realized that the fear came from more than concern.

It came from love.

Suddenly the door burst open and Ivan came through, his gun raised.

"The window."

Ivan nodded and shouted an order to the guards outside the door before turning back to Jarek. He noted the blood on his king's shirt, down low on his right side. "Are you all right, Your Majesty?"

"Superficial," Jarek snapped, more angry at himself, then the guard.

Quamar stepped into the room, his gun raised. "Are you all right, Sarah?"

"Yes, only a little shaken."

Quamar holstered his gun, then glanced at the blood. He grabbed a phone from his pocket and punched a number.

"I need Doctor Haddad at the palace. King Jarek's office. It doesn't matter, either one," he added, then snapped his phone shut.

Jarek placed his gun on his desk and walked over to the window. "The shot pierced the bullet resistant glass. Whoever did this is long gone." He ripped off his shirt, used the clean portion to stem the flow of blood.

Sarah gasped. In the sunlight, she could see the scars, their ugly pattern of ridges and crevices. "Jarek—"

"Don't, Sarah. They are just scars. No more than that. They don't hurt, for God's sake."

"Still, you haven't forgotten for one minute that they are there or forgotten who put them on you."

Jarek hissed softly. No one had said that to him. Ever. No one dared.

"I will check the perimeter," Quamar commented, obviously deciding to leave them alone.

Sarah waited until Quamar left before approaching Jarek. "Please tell me about it."

"I'm sure you've read all the news reports and files," he replied.

"Actually, I didn't." Sarah wanted to stroke the damaged skin, soothe the hurt that had happened so long ago. Instead, she settled on stroking his forearm. "Someone must have kept that fact hidden."

"I was caught unaware." Jarek thrust his fingers through his hair in frustration. "The attack came in the middle of the night. Half my guards had joined the Al Asheera. It made it easy for them to infiltrate the palace grounds."

"And Saree? Was she with you?" Sarah tried to sound nonchalant. But she wanted to know about his wife.

"She'd gone to check on Rashid. He was almost a year at the time and teething. I went to find her but couldn't. The next thing I remember is waking up in a cell beneath the palace."

"But Rashid was saved by Anna—"

"Anna and Saree had been friends since college. Anna had come out here to visit. A vacation of sorts," Jarek explained. "Rashid's nanny saw Anna in the hallway and gave her Rashid. Her name was Alma. She was an old woman. She had been my nanny, then my son's. Anyway, she had no strength left in her bones and couldn't run with a young baby. Instead, she created a diversion to give Anna a chance to escape."

Jarek tightened his jaw against the memory. "They killed Alma after she refused to reveal Rashid's whereabouts."

"That's when Quamar found Anna and Rashid." Sarah remembered the stories. The couple had hidden for several days in the desert with Rashid.

"Yes. He found her in the tunnels beneath the palace. Quamar took her and the baby to his father, Sheik Bari," Jarek explained. "My uncle travels with his people in the desert but changes his route every year. He never gives anyone but myself and Quamar the directions. The Al Asheera had no way of knowing where Quamar had gone."

"And they tortured you to find out where Quamar had taken Rashid and Anna."

"Yes."

"You didn't tell them." There was no doubt in Sarah's mind. Jarek had suffered at the hands of his enemy.

"No," Jarek admitted. "I didn't tell them."

"I wouldn't have, either."

Jarek smiled, a small wry lift of his mouth, at the venom in her voice. "No, I don't imagine you would. Not if they held your child."

"Not my child," Sarah corrected. "Rashid." When he said nothing, she continued. "I love your son, Jarek. I tried not to, but he was just too hard to resist. I will do as you ask and stay away from him when I can. But I won't be rude to him and I won't have his feelings hurt. I won't do that to any child."

Jarek shook his head. "Sarah, I—"

"What happened after Quamar reached his father?" She cut him off, not wanting another argument.

Jarek gave in. "Within a few days, Quamar returned with help from Ian MacAlister and a few other friends from the American government. They managed to free me, but by the time it was all done, Saree had died and so had my uncle, Hassan. My father's brother."

"And a little thief."

Jarek smiled. "Yes. A little thief. His name was Farad. He died saving Anna from Za—" Jarek stopped and shook his head. "It doesn't matter."

"No, I suppose it doesn't," Sarah agreed cautiously, but her mind raced around Jarek's slip. Zahid? Jarek's cousin? If Zahid was going to kill Anna, that meant that he was behind the rebellion.

Before she could ask, Quamar stepped into the room and tossed Jarek a clean shirt. "I think we've found our explosive expert."

"Looks like someone left you a present, Your Majesty," Sandra Haddad murmured.

Jarek turned the body over and noted the gaping throat wound. "Do we know him?"

"Roldo Costa." Sandra handed the card to Jarek. "His wallet identification. By the looks of the rigor mortis, he's been dead for at least twenty-four hours. Probably closer to thirty-six. I'll know for sure once I get him into my lab."

"That would make him dead before the plane blew up yesterday," Sarah pointed out.

"The plane could have been booby-trapped long before we arrived."

"You think he has something to do with Ramon's death?" Sandra reached into her bag and pulled out a camera. Systematically, she took pictures of the dead man.

Sarah turned away. "Maybe our questions yesterday prompted his murder."

"Or maybe he failed. If he'd been hired to blow us up

at the plane, or capture us, he didn't do his job." Jarek picked up the high-powered sniper rifle.

"Every lead I followed on him yesterday, came to a dead end," Quamar admitted, disgusted.

"If it helps at all, Quamar," Sandra took a picture of the throat wound, "Ramon had cancer. Inoperable cancer. I'd diagnosed it a few weeks back. In fact, I was getting ready to pull his airplane license, but he asked me to wait. He didn't want to worry you until he was left no choice."

"How long will it take for you to get me more specifics?"

"A few hours," she replied, before letting her gaze drop to the bloodstain on his fresh shirt. "After I take care of your side."

QUAMAR WALKED INTO Jarek's private quarters. Found his cousin out on the balcony.

"Do you remember when Zahid talked us into the tunnels and then set that fire?" Jarek studied the city laid out below him. His people. His responsibility. "How old were we? Ten? Twelve?"

"Old enough to never trust him again," Quamar stated wryly. "Even then he wanted you dead."

Zahid had been the one with the whip. The one who primarily used it on Jarek, demanding answers. "If I had figured it out sooner, I might have saved myself these scars."

"I pulled Sandra's medical file on Ramon." Quamar held up the file, then tossed it onto a nearby glass covered table. "The cancer had moved to his bones and liver. He would have lived another six months, maybe eight. No more, Sandra said."

"Something has been bothering me." Jarek flipped open the folder, not really seeing the documents as he fingered through them. "When Ramon came in over the desert, he brought the plane low. At first I thought he might have been showing Sarah a closer look at the Sahara but now I'm not so sure. She said she'd been flying all night and had fallen asleep. She hadn't realized they'd been hit until they'd already started in the dive."

"So you believe now that Ramon planted that device in Sarah's purse?"

"I think it's a strong possibility. He had no reason to fly so close to the ground. I considered Ramon family, but if he was going to die soon…" Jarek let the thought trail off, unwilling to put his theory into words. "Zahid. Uncle Hassan. They too were family and still they betrayed us."

"As did others," Quamar added, following his cousin's thoughts.

Jarek nodded. "I want Ramon's bank accounts seized. I want them checked and his apartment searched, Quamar. If Ramon was a traitor, I want to know it by the end of the day."

"I also have been thinking, Jarek," Quamar commented. "Did you not tell me that when Jon first proposed this meeting with Sarah, you were against it? Mainly, because Sarah had proved to have the reputation of being cold-blooded when getting her stories."

"Yes. That and the fact I didn't want to face the past," Jarek admitted. "Why?"

"I have not seen that behavior, that's all," Quamar noted. "What I've seen is the same behavior she took when she told us about Lara Mercer. Her intention had been to expose Lara's relationship with Ian, but when Lara was injured, Sarah's only concern was for Lara herself."

"You're saying she became emotionally involved with her story."

"Ian said that the two women are extremely close."

Quamar made a mental note to make a few calls. The president was a wily old man. Much like his own father, Bari. Quamar wouldn't have put it past Jon Mercer to have done a little matchmaking.

"Since your return from the desert, she has not worried about the story so much as she has about your people. And you. And your son."

"She could be a very good actress."

"True," Quamar agreed reluctantly. "But there is one thing for sure that she is not."

"And what is that?"

"She is not Saree."

Chapter Fourteen

Taer's royal ballroom boasted of smoky blue marble floors and swan-white vaulted ceilings. Their gilded arches, beautifully sloped and adorned wih crystal chandeliers. Imported, Sarah had been told by Nashemia, from Italy over two hundred years before.

The dance floor was crushed with people. Most dressed in black, white or the occasional ivory and blue of the older generation. The more daring wore shades of red that stood out as a sporadic dot amongst four hundred people.

Thin windows stretched from the floor along the outside wall. Ten feet tall and swathed in sapphire velvet with gold trim, several opened up to a large terrace or the royal garden just beyond.

Relieved, Sarah spotted an endless stream of guests still arriving through a doorway harbored with a metal detector archway. Obviously, Quamar and Jarek were not taking any chances on the security.

The ball had started long before Sarah made her way through the doors. Since she wasn't one of the honored guests, she hoped that her late arrival went unnoticed.

"CHAMPAGNE?"

Sarah turned, surprised.

"Here, take it," Sheik Bari Al Asadi handed her the fluted glass. "I hear that champagne goes to some people's heads. Makes them do foolish things."

"Thank you," Sarah said, her lips twitching. "I'll try to remain civilized." She took a sip, enjoyed the bite against her tongue.

Sheik Bari Al Asadi held up a glass of amber liquid, barely visible from inside a large, meaty fist. "If you want civilized, you should drink Scotch, Miss Kwong."

At six feet tall, Sheik Bari carried his age well. And although the photos Sarah kept on file were of a younger Bari, his long, lean frame hadn't changed much over the years.

His once thick, black hair had long ago turned silver and hard-earned crevices mapped his face. The result of years spent outdoors in the unforgiving elements, she imagined. But it was the smaller lines that crinkled at the edge of his eyes that told Sarah a little about the man underneath.

"Would that be MacAlister whiskey, by any chance?" she teased, a little surprised that Bari drank at all.

Bari stared at her for a moment, then laughed. A boom of a laugh that startled more than a few people in the vicinity and started a scurry of conversation.

"As a matter of fact, it's not." Bari winked charmingly. "But only because Jarek's supply was low. And what little he had, I've already taken for my own personal use later. One must have a vice or two, don't you think? To keep life interesting."

"Yes. I believe I do." She raised her glass to his for a silent toast. "Are you visiting long, Sheik Bari?"

"I am only here for a day or so, then I return to where

I belong. With my people." He paused, taking in her coiffed hair and bandaged arm. Finding the contrast curious.

So this is the woman that had caught his nephew's eye. He had heard things from those in the palace—those that still felt it their duty to keep him informed.

Things that intrigued him enough to find out the truth himself.

"I've heard that we came close to meeting the other day," he said casually, feeling little guilt over his tactics.

"Yes, we had a slight problem with the Al Asheera. But we managed."

Pleased that she brushed off the experience with little comment and less drama, Bari couldn't resist prodding just a bit.

"Saving my grandnephew is more than a slight problem, Sarah." Taking advantage of his position, he bypassed etiquette and used her first name. "Our family owes you a great debt."

They both knew what he offered. It would be hard for him to deny any request from her now that he said the words.

"You owe me nothing, Sheik Bari," Sarah replied, her pride hitching her chin high enough to make a statement without being insulting. "I did what needed to be done to protect a child."

INTEGRITY. Courage. Kindness. Sarah Kwong had all three. Shen raised his daughter well, Bari summarized.

"Jarek seems concerned over this agreement with Jon Mercer. This need for publicity," Bari prodded, then covered a hint of a smile by taking a sip of whiskey.

He caught Jarek's profile out of the corner of his eye and understood his nephew enough to know that Jarek was keenly aware of their conversation. Bari gave himself five minutes before his nephew made his way across the floor.

"Jarek has more important issues that require his attention than words I might put to a piece of paper," she responded evenly.

A flash of temper sharpened her green eyes, tightened her mouth. But it was the hurt that stiffened her shoulders, which intrigued him.

The feelings were deeper than he first thought between the two. Only those who cared could be wounded by mere words.

Obviously, their path would not be an easy one. If love was genuine, it had a penchant to torment those affected. But when conquered and embraced, Bari mused, there was nothing more exquisite on this side of paradise.

Hadn't it been that way with his Theresa?

"You will have to come visit my small caravan before you leave," he decided, already anticipating the wedding and more grand nephews and nieces.

One of the greatest pleasures of being old.

"I would like that very much, Sheik Bari," Sarah replied, smiling. He hadn't asked, but ordered. But still with her words, she turned his command into a request.

Bari laughed once more, charmed by her impertinence. "Good, good. I'll have Quamar make the arrangements."

He also made a mental note to press his son, Quamar, for more details. And if that failed, he would call Jon Mercer himself. His connections with world leaders had not lessened after he abdicated his throne. They just remained private meetings between friends.

"ARRANGEMENTS FOR WHAT, Uncle?" Jarek interrupted. When Bari raised his eyebrow, Jarek realized he hadn't quite kept the irritation from his voice.

"Your Majesty." Sarah gave him a small curtsy.

"Sarah."

Moss-green satin skimmed her slender frame, leaving her back bare from the nape of her neck to the delicate concave just beneath her spine.

She wore her hair swept up in an elegant French twist that left the long, graceful slope of her neck exposed to the many masculine eyes in the room.

Jarek had given carte blanche to Anna when she ordered Sarah's wardrobe. But at this moment, he didn't know whether to thank her or curse her for doing the job so well.

"Your ball seems to be a success, Your Majesty."

"And how would you know, Miss Kwong, since you've only just arrived?" he questioned.

"You…you watched for me?" Surprise flickered across her features, made her stutter.

"No," he lied without qualm. Jarek found her discomfort quite charming and made a mental note to do it again sometime soon.

Bari coughed lightly. "I've invited Sarah to visit me when she is finished here, Jarek."

"With the caravan?" He shook his head. "That is impossible. It is too dangerous with the Al Asheera active in the desert."

"You believe I cannot keep Sarah safe?" The rebuke came swiftly, but with no anger. Bari nodded toward the bandage on Sarah's arm. "You could do better?"

"Yes," Jarek responded tightly, but a flush of embarrassment crept up the back of his neck. He didn't need to be reminded of what happened on the cliff. "Jon Mercer has made Miss Kwong's safety my responsibility."

"I can take care of myself. And I have already agreed to Sheik Bari's invitation," Sarah added evenly. "But I appreciate your concern."

"Maybe if you appreciated my position, we wouldn't be having this discussion—"

Suddenly, Rashid broke from the crowd. "Hello, Grandpa Bari. Papa."

"Rashid." Bari hugged the young boy to his side.

Sarah noticed the sheen of tears in the older man's eyes as he kept the prince close just a moment longer than necessary.

In spite of the tough demeanor, it was obvious Bari loved his family and his people.

Rashid pulled away from the embrace, quickly, as young boys tended to do. "You look beautiful, Sarah."

"Thank you, Your Highness." Sarah performed a deep, formal curtsey. "You look pretty handsome yourself," she said, then winked.

"May I have this dance?" The little boy's shyness caught at her chest. "I've been taking lessons."

"I would be honored," she replied softly.

When Rashid held out his arm, Sarah wrapped her hand underneath. With a smile, he escorted her onto the dance floor.

He stopped in the middle, then after a small nod to the orchestra, he bowed. Sarah curtsied.

"He planned this. Look, the orchestra is changing their music," Bari observed with a small chuckle. "He must have been practicing this particular piece with his dancing instructor."

Rashid took her left hand in his, then rested his other

on the soft curve of her waist. Gently, she placed her hand on his shoulder.

The room quieted into a thoughtful murmur as one by one, the guests stopped and watched the young prince lead the American journalist in a flawless waltz.

"My Theresa used to say that few moments were more beautiful than a desert at dawn or more precious than the new day it brought with it," Bari murmured. "I think if she were watching your son and Sarah right now, she would agree that this is one of those moments."

Jarek didn't argue, couldn't if he had wanted to. A rush of emotion clogged his throat, making any statement impossible.

When the dance had ended, Jarek excused himself.

Because he was king—and because he rarely did— Jarek disregarded protocol and joined his son and Sarah on the dance floor. Jarek caught the surprise in Sarah's gaze, and the small tightening of her hand around Rashid's shoulder.

Did she think to protect his son from him?

"Impressive, Rashid." Jarek bowed his head to his son. "I think you've charmed most of the ladies here at the ball."

Rashid glanced around his father, his eyes widening. "I do not have to dance with them, do I, Papa?"

Jarek smiled, understanding his son's sentiment. "No, you do not. Not at least until you are older and it becomes your duty."

Rashid nodded, his brows knitted. "If it is my duty, I will perform it without complaint, Papa."

Jarek patted his son's head. "Well right now, the only thing you have to do is find your Grandpa Bari. He wants to talk with you some more."

Jarek, too, had noticed the tears in his uncle's eyes. The slight reluctance to let the young prince go.

"I will find him." Rashid turned to Sarah and gave her a deep bow. "Thank you for the dance, Sarah."

She bowed her head. "A pleasure, Your Highness."

Rashid raced across the floor. Both Sarah and Jarek laughed. "Sometimes I forget he's only six," she mused.

"Yes, so do I," Jarek admitted, before offering his arm. "May I have this next dance, Sarah?"

When she hesitated, he whispered teasingly, "Afraid?"

"No." But her back stiffened, telling him she wasn't happy.

The orchestra struck up another lovely waltz and he swept her out onto the dance floor.

"We've got an audience," she observed. Once again, they had drawn attention from the guests.

"You had a bigger one with my son."

"I guess I did," she mused.

"May I ask you something?" Jarck asked, just before he led her into a slight whirl.

"Yes."

"When I walked up to you and Rashid, you placed your arm around him as if to protect him from me. Did you think I was going to punish him for dancing with you?"

"I wasn't sure," Sarah admitted, honestly. "I know you've forbidden my socializing with him."

"I wanted you to stay away from him to protect him Sarah, not to hurt him," Jarek explained. "Although I think I failed on both counts. Already he's grown to love you. It will hurt him when you leave."

"It will hurt us both, I think."

Jarek realized there wasn't really any way to avoid the inevitable separation.

"You dance very well."

With relief, she welcomed the change of subject. "Thank you. My parents take the occasional Alaskan cruise, so they can dance the night away aboard a ship. And get free lessons."

Jarek chuckled, catching Sarah by surprise.

"I've seen quite a bit of you during my research. Never have I seen you smile. Or laugh," she commented, her gaze on the curve of his mouth. "You should do it more often."

"A smile is very personal, sometimes even intimate. Something I tend to keep hidden from the outside world."

Sarah stiffened. "Well, that certainly put me in my place."

"I'm sorry. I didn't mean it as an insult, Sarah."

"It's not entirely your fault," she admitted on a sigh. "I think when it comes to you, I've become hypersensitive."

"You really do have the world fooled, don't you?" Jarek murmured, finally understanding what Quamar was telling him earlier that day.

"How so?"

"By reputation, you are a tough, hard-bitten reporter."

"I can be."

"But you're not. Outside your skin is like fine silk," Jarek murmured, next to her ear, enjoying the shiver that raced through her. "When you don't think people are looking, you wear your heart on your sleeve."

"Somehow I don't feel you are paying me a compliment, Your Majesty."

"I'm not sure I am," Jarek agreed. "You must leave, Sarah. Soon, before what started in your bedroom and continued in my office cannot be controlled."

"You want me, but you don't like me, is that it?"

"I don't dislike you. I just cannot have you," Jarek replied. "It would be impossible."

"Not impossible. But complicated. We're not talking marriage here. Or even a long-term affair," Sarah reasoned. "Is this all because of your late wife? Do you still love her?"

"No." Jarek stiffened. "This has nothing to do with her."

But his reaction told her something different. There were feelings there, deep feelings. "If you really think that, then you are not as intelligent as I thought you were, Your Majesty."

The song ended and Sarah deliberately stepped out of his arms and curtsied. "Thank you for the dance, Your Majesty."

"Sarah," he warned, keeping a firm hold on her hand. "You cannot leave the floor angry, or we will draw unwanted attention."

Sarah nodded once, telling him she understood, but the hand on his arm curled in anger as they stepped to the side of the dance floor.

"Your Majesty, may I interrupt?"

The man was slender in build, with thinning brown hair and dull brown, heavy-lidded eyes.

"Miss Sarah Kwong. I'd like you to meet Murad Al Qassar. Murad owns the shipping company that handles all of our crude oil."

"Mr. Al Qassar."

"It is a pleasure, Miss Kwong." He kissed her fingers. Sarah had to resist the urge to tug her hand away. "I'm glad I could talk to you both together and offer my apologies."

"Apologies?"

"I was informed today that one of my employees, Roldo Costa, made an attempt on your lives."

"Not quite. Roldo Costa had been murdered. His body was left at the palace wall. But whoever fired that rifle was very much alive."

"Rest assured I will be performing a complete investigation into this matter, Your Majesty. And I will keep you informed of any progress we make," Murad insisted.

"You can notify my cousin, Quamar, of any details you uncover."

"As you wish." Murad's gaze slipped to the bandage on Sarah's arm. "I had heard that you saved our young prince from certain death out in the desert. Obviously, it is true."

"The story sounds more dangerous than it really was," Sarah replied tactfully.

"You are being modest, Miss Kwong. Those of us who live here know that small children are more vulnerable to the dangers of the desert. Prince Rashid was very lucky you were there to protect him," Murad said, before looking at the king. "Both of you."

"Yes, he was," Jarek agreed, not wanting to be reminded again of how he'd almost lost them both. "My apologies, Murad, but I promised Miss Kwong a stroll through the garden."

"I understand, Your Majesty. It is a beautiful garden," Murad responded, then quickly bowed his head. "A pleasure meeting you, Miss Kwong."

"Thank you," she replied, her smile stiff.

Neither man remarked on the fact that she did not return the compliment.

"WHAT DO YOU THINK Papa said to her? She looks angry." Rashid watched his father and Sarah leave the dance floor.

"What makes you think she's angry?"

"Her eyes get squinty when Papa makes her mad."

"Really?" Bari studied the couple for a moment and had to agree with his nephew. Sarah Kwong wasn't happy. But that wasn't as telling as Rashid's question.

"So what plans are you hatching, young man?" Bari asked.

Rashid glanced up at him. "I'm not planning anything, Grandpa. I was just watching Sarah and Papa."

Bari smiled, but he wasn't fooled. The boy was a carbon copy of Jarek and Bari's brother, Makrad. And more clever than both together.

Makrad would be proud.

"You like her, don't you?"

"Yes. She is my friend now," Rashid answered easily, secure in the knowledge. "Even if she doesn't like Papa."

"And what does that mean, exactly?"

"She promised to always be my friend," Rashid confessed. "I told her that Papa and I don't have friends."

"I think she likes your papa, too," Bari suggested, understanding. Being Royal tended to isolate. It was the nature of the beast.

"How can you tell?"

"A guess." Bari wiggled his eyebrows at his great nephew. "But a very good guess."

Rashid nodded in understanding. After all, he was following the same guess. "She is leaving soon."

"Yes, your papa told me."

"Maybe if he had time to get to know her more, he'd ask her to stay longer."

"What are you thinking, Rashid?"

"You loved Grandma Theresa very much. Everyone says so."

"They do?"

"Yes," Rashid insisted. "They said you loved her so much, you made Grandpa Makrad king so you could be with her in the desert. That's why my papa became king."

"Your papa was destined to be king no matter what, child. Just as you are destined to be, after your papa."

Rashid nodded, accepting what he'd known since birth. "Uncle Quamar told Papa that one cannot fight their destiny."

"He is right."

Rashid smiled, then watched his father take Sarah out to the garden. "Uncle Quamar said sometimes destiny needs something else, too."

"And what is that?"

"A helping hand."

Chapter Fifteen

Jarek led Sarah over the terrace and down into the garden. Within moments the stuffiness of the crowded room slipped away.

The evening was cool, the moon high, but the stars—normally far away—seemed closer, almost within touching distance.

"I don't remember asking for a stroll." Her comment was just short of accusing, the sting of rejection still not forgotten from a few minutes earlier.

"Really? I must have been mistaken," Jarek replied easily, then with a quick nod, commanded Ivan and another Royal Guard to give them some privacy.

Within moments, the guards blocked the path, giving the couple respite from the outside world.

Restless, she stepped toward a bank of blue blossoms nearby. "Borage. The starflower." She cupped the soft triangular petals in her palm, let the sweet scent drift over her.

"I've walked past these flowers a million times and had no idea."

Sarah ignored his teasing. "My mother is a gardener. And although I don't share her passion, I do share the appreciation."

A quiet sense of longing seeped into her bones, undermining her anger, catching Sarah off guard.

"What is it?"

"A flash of homesickness," she admitted warily.

"Understandable," Jarek replied. "We are a long way from Las Vegas. And from what I've seen, you are very close to your parents."

"How? Oh…my file," Sarah remembered. Not wanting to think about his research, she thought about her own. "Your parents were killed in a car accident, weren't they? Right before Rashid was born."

"A personal question?"

"A personal interest," she countered with a quiet dignity. "One that I promise to keep off the record."

"This is personal, isn't it, Sarah? What's happening between us?" He broke off a blossom and tucked it behind her ear. "No matter how much we try to deny it, I think."

Uncomfortable, she reached for the flower. But his hand caught hers. "Let it be," he said, drawing her hand to his chest. "It suits you."

"Tell me about your parents, Jarek."

"My father was a passionate man. About his people, his country, the land. He was a good man. Fair, honorable," Jarek told her, the love evident in his tone. "But my mother was the true diplomat—the quiet strength behind my father. Theirs was an arranged marriage that eventually became a loving marriage."

"They sound a lot like my parents." Not once did Jarek mention his father the king, only the man.

"There isn't a day that goes by that I don't miss them."

"I don't know how you survived losing so many, Jarek," Sarah wondered out loud.

"Bari and Quamar are my family. Anna and their children, also," Jarek replied. "And of course, Rashid."

"Bari is your father's brother, isn't he?"

"Yes. Bari is the oldest son, then my father, Makrad, and then Hassan," Jarek explained. "But Bari fell in love with a Christian woman—Theresa Bazan. You might have heard of her. Quamar told me she had worked with your father many years ago."

Sarah frowned. "I'll have to ask him. I don't remember her."

"When Bari's father objected to Theresa, Bari abdicated the throne to my father."

"So Quamar would've been king?"

"At the time, no. He is illegitimate. Bari never married Theresa."

"At the time? Do you think his illegitimacy wouldn't matter now?"

"Taer is changing," Jarek replied, his thumb absently stroked her wrist. "For better or worse, it is catching up quickly with the modern world and ideas."

"It must be hard to watch the change that's coming to your people, the country." Unable to deal with the flutter and heat from his caress, Sarah tugged her hand away and hugged her arms to her chest. More for protection than the chill of the air, she turned away.

The desert was no more than a black sea of shadows beyond the lights of the city.

"There is something almost magical about Taer, isn't there?" she wondered out loud. "I've lived near the Mojave Desert most of my life. But I couldn't describe a single landscape to you. But the Sahara is different, isn't it? It's almost as if it's a living, breathing thing."

Jarek slipped off his dinner jacket and placed it over her

shoulders. When he pulled the lapels close, masculine fingers brushed across the hollow of her throat, lingered just long enough for her breath to catch, her knees to tremble.

As if sensing her momentary weakness, he pulled her back into his chest and tightened his arms around her.

Because she loved, because she needed—Sarah accepted, and allowed her body to soften.

"There is a belief in my family that the Sahara is a woman," Jarek murmured.

"Anna told me."

"Did she tell you the Sahara fascinates the men of Taer?" His warmth seeped through the jacket, taking the chill away, thawing the rest of her resistance. "With a female's scent, textures and temperaments." His lips skimmed the nape of her neck.

"Serene. Unpredictable. Dangerous. She draws men in." His fingers followed his mouth, kneading the tense muscles for a moment. Slowly, he turned her around, taking his time as he pulled her back to him. "She tests their endurance, tempts them to do things they wouldn't do normally."

"Does she tempt you?" she whispered. Her hands moved up his chest, over thin material of his shirt until his heart beat beneath her palm. Strong. Steady.

"Yes." The word rolled over her in one, long, raspy drawl.

Desire hit, a flash of heat that set her skin sizzling, her insides churning.

"With her scent," Jarek whispered next to her ear. His breath hot against the delicate shell. Her fingers curled into his chest.

"And her softness." His thumb skimmed the smooth skin just under her jaw, traced the slender curve of her neck. "Her taste." His mouth hovered over hers, their breath mingling. Warm, moist.

His kiss wasn't gentle. He'd teased them both too long for gentle. Made them suffer too much.

Deep, wet, blistering, his mouth took hers.

The jacket fell to the ground, forgotten. His arms tightened, bringing her up to his chest—not satisfied until her breasts pressed against him.

His hands moved over her, kneading her shoulders, tracing her spine, sliding his fingers beneath the material at its base. Giving into the urge from the dance floor, his fingers dipped to the soft curve of her bottom, stroking the lace beneath.

Sarah gasped against his mouth. Suddenly, she stretched, then shifted. On tiptoe, she snaked her arms around his neck, insistent. Her mouth was wild, erotic. Her body moved against his, restless and throbbing.

When his hand cupped her breast, she whimpered as her desire wound to a fever pitch. Suddenly, his mouth broke from hers. It moved nipping, then soothing, first down her neck across her shoulder then back to the hollow of her collarbone.

Sarah shifted back, giving him more access. He tugged at her bodice, freeing her breast to the night air. Sarah shivered, the clash of heat and cold almost too much to bear. She yanked his hair, urging his mouth down to her breast, craving relief to her torment.

"Your Majesty." Trizal's voice cut through the night air. Jarek stiffened against Sarah, his body instantly tight, a steel band coiled way beyond its breaking point.

Still, he held her close, hiding her nakedness in the garden shadows. He forced his hands to soothe, rather than incite.

"What is it?" Jarek snapped out the words, the harshness more from desire and self-directed anger than from the other man's timing.

"My apologies, Your Majesty. But they need you at the hospital. It is Bash. He died less than an hour ago."

MURAD STUDIED THE CONVERTIBLE as it turned into the construction site and parked a few yards away. Floodlights spilled from the warehouse docks. Their glare cast a jaundice hue over the labyrinth of steel beams and columns that shaped the first phase of his high-rise.

Anticipation had his eyes lingering over the steel supports that rose above the warehouse district, but it was vanity that made him count the floors. With sixty in all—including the corporate penthouse—the Qassar building topped the tallest high-rise in the city by more than forty floors.

Murad had to give Jarek credit. He'd moved Taer into the 21st century and put their small country on the international map. As the overseas interest increased, trade expanded, high-rises would soon be the norm—forcing the city boundaries out and international magnates to take notice.

A man could get rich, if he played his money right and got in at the ground.

And Murad had already hit the ground running.

"Don't you ever get tired of looking at this damn building?" Oruk stepped out of his car and shut the door.

"No."

"Dreaming about the logo on top?"

Murad's lips twisted into a rare smile. "Actually, I was dreaming of Taer's gross national product increase over the next twenty years."

"I hope that's not why I'm out here talking to you and freezing my best parts off."

"No, you're out here because you sliced a man's throat—a man who you insisted I put on my payroll—then dumped his body at Jarek's front door." Murad leaned back against his car and crossed his arms. "I want to know why."

Murad's voice was crisp, business-like, but Oruk wasn't fooled. He'd worked with Murad long before anyone had ever heard of Al Qassar Shipping. Hell, most of the money that Oruk paid him in illegal arms shipment fees started Al Qassar Shipping.

"Don't act like you're upset that Roldo is dead. He failed to kill the king and the prince." Oruk waved a hand, dismissing the other man's fit of temper. "He was becoming a liability, shooting his mouth off at the Cathouse. I was left little choice."

"You could've tossed him into the desert for the buzzards. Never to be seen again," Murad argued, then jabbed his thumb at the framed building behind him. "You could have even given his body to me and I would have buried it in six feet of concrete and steel."

"Yes, but then Jarek's people would be knocking on your door, hunting for Roldo and we would risk them uncovering something else. Something more damaging to our plans. This way they have him already and all they can do is ask questions."

"Of me," Murad snapped.

"So you provide the answers on whatever you *might* know," Oruk indicated. "It's not like you're involved in the day-to-day business of the drill site. You have more than enough employees—use them to bog things down a bit."

"And the guard's death? The man called Bash?"

"Consider him at the right place. At the right time."

"What the hell is that suppose to mean?"

"Bash has no connection to you, so why are you worried? His death will just throw off the investigation on Roldo."

"Roldo had better be the last loose end, Oruk," Murad stated. "Ever since the plane crash, Jarek has more than doubled the palace and the drilling site security. Killing him now would be suicide."

"Not if we have a person to take the fall."

"Who?"

"The woman reporter," Oruk suggested slyly.

"You're out of you mind," Murad retorted. "When the news came of Bash's death, Jarek's secretary found them out in the garden together. Alone."

"My spies tell me Jarek still suspects her over the tracking device found in her purse," Oruk commented. "You and I both know he has no reason to trust a woman. A few more pushes in her direction—"

"You're willing to bet a billion dollars on Jarek's hatred for women?" Murad scoffed.

"No." Oruk pulled a small digital tape recorder out of his pocket and stroked the bullet crease in its side. "Just this woman."

SARAH STOOD AT THE BEDROOM window, watching the driveway just past the courtyard.

Periodically she caught glimpses of her reflection in the glass. The pale skin, the dark smudges beneath her eyes—eyes that glistened with tears when she lost her grip on the worry and fear that ebbed just beneath the surface.

Time bled through the night, until one hour became four. In the first hour, Nashemia came in with tea and soup. Once the servant assured Sarah that she was holding up in spite of the news of Bash's death, Nashemia urged

Sarah to eat. But soon the servant gave up after she realized Sarah's only interest lay outside the window.

Sarah wrapped Jarek's coat tighter, hugging her arms to her chest, taking comfort in the scent of leather and spice. Behind her, Sarah heard the hiss and crackle of the fire that Nashemia lit before she'd left. But the heat of the flames did little to take the chill from Sarah's bones.

The news of Bash's death had traveled quickly through the palace. Ivan had returned to his post outside her door, but the young man's shoulders weren't as steady, his stance not as tall.

She wanted to be at the coroner's office with Jarek, asking questions, demanding answers. But it wasn't her country, her people, or her right.

Jarek wasn't even her man.

The soft muffle of voices drifted through the door. Questions were asked, then answered in unintelligible murmurs.

Sarah stood by the window, her eyes locked on the handle as it turned, her breath tight in her chest.

The door opened. She caught a glimpse past Jarek's shoulder, enough to see that Ivan was no longer posted outside.

Jarek stepped through, turned around and quietly shut the door. When he turned back his gaze was level, the shadows in his eyes, haunted. He waited with his hand on the lock, giving her plenty of time to object.

Never before had he looked more like a warrior. His stance wide, his body rigid, his features set. Beneath hooded eyes, his black irises glittered, sharp with need, desire and, she thought sadly, fury.

"Bash?"

"Later." He shook his head, visibly pushing back the rage. "I need it to be later."

When she nodded, Jarek almost sighed in relief.

Then, with the snap of the bolt, the demons of the past and present receded to their dark corners. And with them they took his uncertainties, his questions and his responsibilities.

"I wasn't sure you'd come to me." Slowly, she slid his jacket from her shoulders and tossed it on a nearby chair. "I'm glad you did."

Jarek forced himself to stand still.

She wore the ball gown from earlier. The satin shimmered in the firelight. The color of dark, liquid emeralds, the dress flowed over her, the material sheathing her body like a second skin.

She'd taken her shoes off. From where he stood, he could see her toes peeking out from beneath the gown.

Slowly, she slipped the straps from her shoulders and pulled her arms through.

"Stop." The word broke from his throat, low and husky—vibrating with forced control.

"All right." The nerves were gone from her voice, replaced with a feminine confidence. Barefooted she walked toward him, the dress clinging to every curve, covering all but the graceful slope of her shoulders.

Sarah stopped when less than six inches separated their bodies. Passion darkened her eyes to a turbulent green— wicked and sultry, they drew him in.

"We'll do this together."

Jarek hissed. Desire rippled through him, tremor upon tremor, and with it the balance of power shifted from him to her.

She took his right hand in both of hers and brought his fingers to her lips. Gently, she kissed each knuckle, little butterfly kisses that made his hand clench, his body tighten.

Laughing softly, she took his middle finger and

stretched it out. The green of her eyes darkened wickedly as she drew his finger into her mouth, running her tongue up, then down its length, nipping, soothing, sucking.

Desire exploded into molten lava. It raced through his veins, nearly brought him to his knees.

"Ready?" Not waiting for an answer, she guided his fingers to her heart. It beat once, twice beneath his palm before she took both of his hands and slipped them over her breasts.

His thumbs brushed her nipples, slick and hard beneath the satin. Her breath deepened, her breasts grew heavy.

Of their own accord, his hands leisurely slid down her body, peeling the satin dress from the silk of her skin. Using his knuckles, he traced the contour of her ribs, her side, the soft hollow where her hip met thigh. His thumb snagged the wisp of lace. With a short tug he snapped the thin material and left it to pool with her dress at their feet.

Sarah swayed into him, and just that quick the balance of power shifted once more.

No longer happy with distance, Jarek slipped his arm beneath her bottom and lifted her up against his chest.

"You're still dressed," she whispered, even as her arms slipped around his neck, her finger buried themselves in the thick of his hair.

He caught one of her nipples in his mouth and suckled until pleasure purred at the back of her throat.

Suddenly, she broke free and slid down the length of his body, arching against him when his hands stroked the base of her spine, the sensitive spot between her shoulder blades.

"My turn." One by one, she undid his shirt buttons, leaving little kisses along the taut skin beneath.

She slipped the shirt just past his shoulders, only to stop when his hands caught her wrists.

"Don't," he whispered, his voice raspy.

"Shh…" She kissed his lips softly, her breath sweet against his mouth. Then with a single tug the shirt fell to the floor.

She kissed his chin. Slid her lips over his collarbone. His hands slipped behind her head, until his fingers tangled in her hair and brought the thick locks tumbling to her shoulders.

The ends brushed his chest as she trailed her mouth across a flat brown nipple, stopping only a moment to tease, before moving on.

Slowly, she kissed the rigid muscle between his neck and shoulder.

Jarek waited, his breath held in check. On her tiptoes, she worked her way around to his back, leaving butterfly kisses across his shoulder, then nape of his neck.

Her hands drifted over his arms, held him tight as she pressed her chest to his back.

Jarek groaned against the bittersweet pleasure that rocked him to the core. It had been a long time since anything other than his shirt had touched the scars.

With lips and fingers, Sarah caressed each ridge, imprinting herself, keeping the demons from seeping back.

Finally, Jarek could take no more. He turned, slid his arm under her legs and picked her up. He cradled her once again against his chest.

His mouth found hers in a slow, sweet, healing kiss that left them both breathless.

With a gentleness he'd never thought himself capable of, he placed her in the middle of the bed.

She rose up on one elbow, her eyes heavy with desire as she watched him shed his pants.

Sarah took in the lean muscle that roped through his frame. The firm thighs, the smooth, sculpted chest.

But it was the longing in the dark eyes that had her lifting her arms.

A moment later, he pressed her into the mattress, imprinting his body against hers. Just as she had done a few minutes before.

He dug deep for the tenderness he had not used for a long time—a tenderness she needed to feel, as much as he needed to give.

As if reading his thoughts, Sarah parted her legs, settling him against the warm, wet apex between.

A low groan erupted from deep within Jarek's chest. The underlying pitch filled with so much emotion that it threatened to crack his heart wide open.

Sarah tugged his hair, pulling his mouth down until it hovered over hers. "I'll make it better, Jarek," she whispered. "I promise."

He kissed her slow at first, letting the hunger build until their mouths moved together. Wild. Erotic.

Jarek's hand slipped down between them to the soft triangle between her legs. He cupped the heat, then used his thumb, moving it in gentle, tender circles until she rocked restlessly against him, wanting more.

She curved her hands over his back, kneading the tense muscles, caressing the quivering, sweaty skin until desire pinched at the base of his spine and every nerve in his body screamed for release.

Underneath, she drew up taut, trembling against him. Her breath came in quick gasps as she fought against the tidal wave that threatened to sweep them over a precipice of control.

"Jarek," she whispered, her eyes fluttered before they locked with his. "I can't. Please."

He drove into her with one, long thrust. Then watched the green in her eyes lose focus with pleasure.

They moved together, the tenderness he'd been afraid to reach for there in every smooth, silky stroke.

For the last time the balance of power shifted, away from both of them.

But neither cared. The freedom far outweighed the risk. They careened toward the edge, exploding over the precipice, out of control. Each held on to the other as they plunged into the peaceful abyss beyond…where only the two of them existed.

Chapter Sixteen

Jarek rose from the bed, careful not to wake Sarah. What he'd done was stupid. He added unnecessary risk to her life.

He could not love her, could not risk her. Could not trust her.

Yet he'd bedded her.

If ever a time he deserved to be whipped, it would be now, he thought with self-deprecation.

He'd spent four hours the night before looking for answers, consoling a devastated family.

Coming up short on both accounts.

He walked past the dresser, only to stop when his gaze fell on her recorder. Without thought, he picked it up and hit the play button.

"Your parents were killed in a car accident, weren't they? Right before Rashid was born."

"A personal question?"

"A personal interest. One I promise to keep off the record."

Jarek pressed the stop button. Then the fast forward. Finally, he hit play.

"There isn't a day I don't think about them."

THE SUN PEAKED through the bedroom curtains, waking Sarah. Automatically, her hand stretched to the pillow beside her. Finding it empty, she sat up and looked around.

"What is this?" Jarek sat in the Queen Anne chair, fully dressed in his clothes from the night before. In his hand, he held her recorder.

"You're kidding, right?" Slowly, she sat up, tugging the comforter above her breasts and brushed her hair behind her shoulder. If she was going to take this punch, she'd lead with her pride. "You know it's my recorder."

"I found it on your dresser."

"You searched my room? After I fell asleep? After we made—"

"Yes." He tossed the recorder into her lap.

"You decided to listen to my notes." She picked up the recorder and offered it back to him. "Feel free, I have nothing to hide."

"Turn it on."

"Why?"

"Do it!" he snapped.

Crestfallen, she hit the switch.

"A personal question?"

"A personal interest. One I promise to keep off the record."

Slowly, Sarah shut the words off. "You think I broke my word."

"Lies." He thrust his fingers through his hair. "I'm tired of them."

So much for the pledges of undying love.

"I didn't record our conversation." Sarah tossed the recorder to the end of the bed.

"I trusted you, damn it."

"You never trusted me. You just slept with me. A person can do that without trust easily enough," Sarah argued dully.

A hiss of anger shot across the room. Jarek took a step forward, his hands fisted.

She gathered the sheet, using the thin material for a veil of protection.

Bitterness edged her laugh, ate at her gut. "You realize when I finally hear what's in your heart, it's nothing but accusations of betrayal."

"Enough." Jarek grabbed her chin until her eyes met his. "I want to know who you're helping."

"No one," Sarah whispered, this time the tear ran unchecked down her cheek. "Not even myself."

"What the hell are you thinking, arresting my reporter?"

Jarek wasn't surprised those would be the first words out of President Jon Mercer's mouth.

"I'm thinking that I have lost four good men. Two who died under suspicious circumstances."

"And you believe Sarah is involved?"

"Yes." Jarek's hand gripped the phone harder. "And until I have answers, she stays under guard."

"What evidence do you have, Jarek?"

"You mean in addition to the tracking bug I found in her purse after the crash?"

"Circumstantial. Anyone could have planted that on her."

"I found her recorder in her bedroom with taped conversations. Private conversations that should not have been in her possession."

"You're out of your mind. Sarah wouldn't break our agreement—" A string of cuss words cut off his sentence. "What were you doing in her bedroom?"

After years of jungle and political warfare, Jon Mercer was no fool. And Jarek knew it.

"You slept with her, didn't you?"

"Yes," Jarek confirmed, the word dug in like barbed wire against his throat.

"And then imprisoned her?"

"I confined her to her room," Jarek responded. He was well within his right. "And before you go there, I didn't sleep with her as some ruse to get information. I didn't discover the recorder until afterward."

President Mercer let out a long whistle. "So you tried and convicted her without getting the facts."

"She wouldn't say anything after I showed her the recordings." Pain sliced deep—deeper than any of the scars that crisscrossed his back.

The fact that he'd allowed himself to care, allowed himself to believe, if only a small bit, scared the hell out of him. And drove him to this one last option.

Mercer continued, unaware of Jarek's struggle for emotional distance. "I cannot believe you think Sarah is behind this."

"I don't," Jarek admitted.

There was a long pause. "I'm not following you, son."

"Look, Jon. Someone is trying really hard to make me believe Sarah is involved. I need to find out who that might be and protect her at the same time."

"So you accused her of treason and locked her up."

It wasn't a question but Jarek chose to answer anyway. "In her suite. It's not like I threw her in jail, damn it," Jarek argued, refusing to second guess his decision. "If I tried to reason with her, she'd make herself a bigger target. This way she's distracted with her anger for me."

"You're in love with the girl, aren't you?"

Jarek ground the answer between his jaw. He would only admit the truth to himself. Making it public wasn't an option.

"Well, I'll be damned."

"I'm glad you find this situation humorous," Jarek bit out, not bothering to contain his impatience.

"Jarek, you're either the bravest son of a bitch I know, or the stupidest," Jon Mercer observed after he got his laughing under control.

"Neither." The word was clipped, his royal breeding reasserting itself. "I am a king who must protect his own. Once I resolve this, she can go home. If she goes home hating me, all the better."

"I don't have to tell you that if this isn't resolved soon, our agreement is going to be in jeopardy, son," Jon pointed out, his voice suddenly serious.

"I would expect no less."

"Good. Then you'll understand why I'm sending Cain MacAlister to Taer to help straighten this mess out. He's already on his way," Jon added. "You have twenty-four hours."

Cain MacAlister was the Director of Labyrinth—an American black-ops agency—Quamar's old boss and one of Jon Mercer's most trusted friends.

"Twenty-four hours for what?"

"To think up an apology."

"I won't need that long," Jarek admitted. "You will have my official apology as soon as I get to the bottom of this."

"Me?" Jon snorted. "You'll need every second of that twenty-four hours to apologize to Sarah. And even then, if I know Sarah, it won't be enough."

HER PRISON WAS LITTLE MORE than her bedroom, but it might as well have been the prison cell Jarek had described in the palace basements.

Sarah choked back the anger. She'd been so stupid to trust someone who was incapable of feeling.

Keys rattled, then the door opened slowly. Ivan stepped back and allowed Nashemia past with a food tray in one hand and a set of white towels in the other.

The young guard refused to make eye contact when he shut the door.

Sarah wasn't angry, understanding Ivan's loyalty was to his king.

"I'm not really hungry, Nashemia."

"You must eat to keep up your strength." The woman glanced back at the door, her features tight with nervousness.

She placed the tray on the coffee table and stepped closer to Sarah. "I do not believe you are the spy, mistress," she whispered.

"Thank you. That means a lot to me."

"I've taken upon myself to arrange for your escape."

"My what?"

"Escape. I've heard that the king refuses to extradite you back to your home. That means you will stand trial here for treason."

"What's the penalty for treason?"

"Death, by firing squad."

"I don't believe—" Sarah stopped and shook her head. Did Jarek hate her that much?

"I've arranged for your escape tonight. I usually bring Ivan a snack and some coffee at midnight. Be ready, then." She reached between the towels and handed Sarah a white servant's dress and scarf to cover her face.

"No, Nashemia, I don't want you to risk—"

"I risk nothing. I must go now." Nashemia grabbed her hand. "Be ready. I will make sure you get to the airport, then home. You can prove your innocence much easier from America."

Before Sarah could say anything, Nashemia was back through the door.

Sarah sat on the bed, gripping the servant's uniform in her fingers, her heart little more than a cold lump in her chest.

Suddenly, she realized there were many forms of death.

THE BUZZER ON JAREK'S DESK was insistent. He hit the button on the intercom. "What is it, Trizal?"

"Your Majesty, Dr. Haddad is here to see you," the secretary answered. "She says it is urgent."

"All right, I'll see her."

Sandra walked in, her khakis and blouse now replaced with doctor's surgical scrubs and a white lab coat. "I just finished Bash's autopsy, Jarek."

"And?"

"Bash died from potassium chloride. A poison that attacks the heart muscle and caused Bash to go into cardiac arrest. His death had nothing to do with his burn injuries."

"He was murdered."

"Yes."

"How long was the poison in his system?"

"Quite a while. Five, maybe six hours. It had been added to his drip, so the poison took time working."

Jarek frowned.

"Whoever entered his room, knew what they were doing," she said.

"Any ideas who?"

"Sarah Kwong."

"Are you sure?" Jarek leaned back in his chair. "She had told me that she'd seen him twice yesterday, but I don't think—"

"Three times," Sandra corrected. "The last time places her in his room around the same time he'd been given the poison."

"How would she have access to enough poison to kill Bash?"

"I don't know," Sandra admitted. "But I do know that she visited Bash just before the Independence Day Ball. I believe that was why she was late."

RASHID'S STOMACH felt funny and tight, like a twisted ball of twine he couldn't unravel. He slid out of his bed and knelt on the floor. He slipped his hand under the bed and pulled a picture that he had taped to the bottom.

He stared at the woman who was smiling in the picture.

His mother, Saree.

The ball tightened. No matter how hard he tried he could not remember her. Or the love he'd felt for her as a baby.

Her long, black hair was thick and straight. Her eyes sparkled and crinkled at the corners when she smiled. The sparkle was something he never found in father's eyes.

Rashid wanted his father to be proud of him, but mostly he just wanted his father.

Sarah loved him. He was sure. He could tell by the way she hugged him. It was like Aunt Anna's hugs, but warmer, more special.

Plus, she listened to him. That always proved adults loved you.

Sometimes it scared Rashid, because his father never did. But Sarah had changed him that way. It seemed that his father noticed Rashid more, not just when he got into trouble.

With a sigh, he put the picture back in place. He didn't want the maids to find it when they made his bed in the morning. If his father discovered the picture, he would take it.

He didn't really miss his mother, but he was sad over her death. Maybe Sarah could change that for them all.

Rashid's stomach growled. He hadn't eaten dinner. He had been too excited about his plans to help destiny.

Quickly, he went to his bedroom door and listened to the low murmuring of his two royal guards. Satisfied the guards were still at their post, he tiptoed to his bathroom and opened the laundry chute.

Maybe he could find a midnight snack in the kitchen.

SARAH PACED HER ROOM, her hands fisted in the caftan pockets. She'd dressed in the white servant clothes less than an hour before, then kept her robe handy just in case Ivan opened the door.

"Mistress Kwong?"

Sarah glanced at the clock. Just after midnight. "I'm here, Nashemia," she whispered and opened the door.

The young woman stepped over the slumped guard. "We must hurry. The sleeping drug I gave Ivan will last a few hours but we could be discovered by any one of the guards or servants."

"We will leave, but first I need to ask if you have seen my jade necklace?"

Nashemia's eyes went to Sarah's neck. "No, mistress. Has it been stolen?"

She'd spent the last hour searching for her necklace. The night before, she had left it in her nightstand, only to find it gone earlier today.

"It doesn't matter. We don't have time. If it turns up, will you save it for me?"

"Yes, I promise."

Sarah nodded and grabbed her bag from the dresser. The recorder caught her eye. She'd thought to leave it behind, but at the last minute she placed it in her caftan pocket. Why give Jarek more ammunition against her?

Slowly, Nashemia opened the door and peered up the corridor. Nodding to Sarah, both women stepped around the sleeping guard and headed toward the rear of the palace.

The halls were nearly deserted with only the occasional guard walking sentry. Quietly, they maneuvered down the stairs and into the back servant quarters.

"Where are we going?"

"I have an SUV," Nashemia answered, her eyes on the darkened rooms. "I will take you over the border. I have family who can help you get back to the States."

Sarah followed the other woman outside the palace walls to a black SUV. Both women were relieved when they reached the car without mishap.

It wasn't until she was at the car that she noticed the emblem on the side. "This is one of the palace vehicles."

"Yes. It was the most accessible." Nashemia opened the door, urging Sarah inside.

"I don't want you to get into trouble. And stealing one of the palace vehicles definitely brings trouble." Sarah frowned and climbed in the front. Then hesitated. What was she doing? Proving herself guilty and taking an innocent bystander along with her?

The servant got into the passenger seat and closed the door.

"Nashemia, I cannot do this. This is wrong. I need to see the king."

"You cannot, mistress." Desperation tinged Nashemia's words. "He will imprison us both."

"I won't tell him how I escaped. I can tell them I shimmied down the laundry vent," she said, mentally thanking Rashid.

"I'm sorry, Mistress Kwong," Nashemia's voice hardened. "But I cannot let you spoil our plans."

"What plans?" Sarah didn't see the scarf, smell the bite of chemical until it was too late.

She struggled but the first whiff of ether was caught on her gasp of surprise. Sarah struggled against the sickening darkness that clawed at her belly, brought bile to the back of her throat.

Her eyes fluttered, focused for a moment on Nashemia's smile. Then there was nothing.

"I WANT TO SEE SARAH NOW, JAREK," Cain MacAlister ordered the moment Trizal escorted him and his two companions into the office.

Jarek nearly smiled over the arrogance. A trait he'd seen many times before. No protocol. No niceties. But in truth, he hadn't expected any.

Cain was the head of an American black-ops division called Labyrinth. And although it had been nearly two years since Jarek had seen his friend, he noted he hadn't changed.

Born with the lean, aristocratic features of his ancestors, raven-black hair and steel-gray eyes, Cain MacAlister was still the best person to have at your side during any emergency.

"Sarah's in her suite under house arrest."

After Cain, came Ian MacAlister, his hand extended. Jarek grabbed his hand and was immediately pulled into a bear hug. "Heard you need help, Your Majesty," Ian said before his brother could respond to the house arrest comment.

Unlike Cain, Ian MacAlister, was more meat and muscle. With light brown hair, laser-blue eyes and at least three days of whiskers, Jarek thought Ian fit the image of a California beach bum, more than a retired government agent.

"Bloody hell, Jarek. Did you need to wait until disaster

struck before you decided to ask for help?" Jordan Beck, the third man, joked and slapped Jarek on the shoulder.

"I didn't ask for help. Jon Mercer decided I needed it," Jarek said wryly. Of the three, Jarek was the closest to Jordan. With a lean frame and sharp features, Jordan was a British blue blood. Born the Earl of Beck, the ex-agent came from a long line of English aristocracy, one that left him twenty-eighth in line to England's throne.

"I'll send for Sarah so you can all see for yourself that she is not being mistreated."

Without warning, Quamar burst into the room. "That will not be possible, Your Majesty."

At one time, Quamar had worked for Cain as a Labyrinth agent. He considered all the men in the room friends, so he did not mince his words.

"Sarah is gone." Quamar glanced at his cousin. "We found Ivan unconscious. And this note on her nightstand."

Jarek ripped open the end of the envelope and pulled out the letter. His eyes quickly scanned the message. "The Al Asheera have no desire to kill the American reporter. We only wish to negotiate with our King."

Jarek tossed the paper onto his desk. "The drilling site. Come alone."

"That's original," Jordan commented dryly.

"And not going to happen," Ian added.

Jarek looked at his friends. "I will take no chances with Sarah's life."

Cain raised an eyebrow. "That sounds personal. Especially for a man who had Sarah under arrest for treason."

"It is personal. Very personal."

"Now I understand why Jon Mercer sent us all here," Cain reasoned. "To keep you from doing something stupid."

"I think he's already done the stupid part." Jordan

whistled softly. "I accused my wife, Regina, of being my father's mistress the first time we met."

"She forgave you," Ian mused.

"Mostly," Jordan answered, then turned to Jarek. "But if I had her arrested? I'd still be sleeping with the dog."

"Shut up, Beck. She was under house arrest. And I did it for her own good," Jarek said gruffly, not letting the other men see what the words did to the knot in his chest. He'd met Regina, a quiet rather soulful woman. Beautiful in a bookish manner. Nowhere near the temperament of his Sarah.

His Sarah.

"That's not the worst of it, Jarek," Quamar warned. "Rashid is missing, too."

"What?"

"Does the note mention him?" Cain asked, frowning.

"No." Fear jarred Jarek's spine, made his hand shake. "Have you searched the grounds?"

"The guards are searching right now." Quamar gestured to the window. "But my gut is telling me—"

"He's with Sarah," Jarek interrupted.

Quamar glanced at the note. "Whether they know it or not."

Chapter Seventeen

Sarah woke to the rumble and bump that echoed the pounding in her head.

"So you decided to join us."

She looked up and saw Murad sipping a glass of wine from a nearby couch. She took in the red velvet, the brocade wall paper, the stained glass lamps.

A train. They were on a train.

"I always thought I was born in the wrong century," he commented, as if reading her thoughts.

"I question the fact that you were born at all," Sarah answered with derision. "More like spawned, maybe."

"Oh, I can assure you I was born." Murad stood, straightened his suit. After taking a moment to brush a piece of lint off of his tie, he stepped over to Sarah.

Without warning, he backhanded her across the face. Pain exploded through her cheek, knocking her off the couch and onto the floor.

"Do you need any more convincing?" Murad gripped her arm, his bony fingers dug into her skin. "Or have you decided to keep your mouth shut?"

Sarah nodded and nearly gagged on the metallic taste of blood against her tongue.

Murad picked her up and shoved her back onto the couch. "Good. I hate to repeat myself." He poured himself more wine from a corner bar and sat back on a nearby settee. "Jarek has been informed of your predicament. We'll see if he comes and saves you."

"He hates me. You're wasting your time if you're using me as a bargaining chip."

"Let me go!" The scream ripped the passenger car. The little hairs on Sarah's neck stood at attention.

The car door burst open and Oruk walked in holding Rashid by his waistband.

"The brat followed her from the palace." With a flick of his wrist, he tossed Rashid against Sarah.

"Sarah." The little boy hugged her.

Sarah's heart skipped a beat. "How did you get here?"

"I heard Nashemia on the phone telling Murad to meet you both at the train. That once she had you, my father would come for you." Rashid looked at Sarah. "I was too late to warn you so I snuck into Nashemia's car." The boy wiped the tears with the back of his hand. "I was going to help you but Nashemia had too many bad guys on the train. One of them caught me climbing from the top of the passenger car."

"Sweet Lord." Her heart jumped to her throat.

"It seems the little prince wants to be your hero, Miss Kwong," Murad observed wryly.

"Sarah, we are going to Papa's drilling site. We are almost there."

"The boy pays attention, doesn't he?" Oruk commented. "Even when he should mind his own business, maybe?" He took his knife out from his boot and pointed it at Rashid. "Sometimes, little boys who eavesdrop get their ears cut off."

"Stop scaring the prince, Oruk." Nashemia walked in.

Gone was the white servant caftan. In its place was a slim-fitting suit, scarlet-red and tailored with enough cleavage and thigh showing to be this side of vulgar, Sarah thought, derisively.

Nashemia sauntered over to the little boy and patted his cheek. "He's too cute to mutilate."

"You've set a trap for my papa, haven't you?" he demanded. The royal in him more apparent than ever.

"Yes," Nashemia admitted, amused. "But don't worry, we won't kill him right away. We need him alive for a while. That's why you and Sarah are so important to us."

Oruk grabbed Rashid's hands and placed them around Sarah's right arm. He bound the boy's wrists together with a plastic zip tie, linking the woman and child together.

"My father will stop you," Rashid threatened.

Nashemia's lips peeled back over her teeth. "I suppose. If I gave him the chance. But that is unlikely."

Sarah shifted, pulling Rashid closer to her.

"You give him more comfort than his mother ever did," Murad observed negligently. He handed Nashemia a glass of wine.

"She is maternal, isn't she?" Nashemia rolled the stem of the wineglass between her fingers. "Too bad Saree never was."

"How do you know my mother?" Rashid demanded.

Nashemia smiled into her wineglass before taking a sip. "I actually know quite a lot about your mother." She glanced at Oruk. "He told me."

Oruk smiled and put away his knife. "Did you know that your father shot your mother dead while she held you in her arms, Rashid?"

Rashid stiffened. "You liar!"

Sarah realized instantly that Oruk told the truth. Jarek's

reactions. His distrust. The fact he never mentioned Saree's name.

"Rashid. Listen to me, not them," Sarah said urgently. "Your father loves you. More than anything on this earth. He was tortured because he wouldn't tell men like Oruk where your uncle Quamar had hidden you."

"But my mother," Rashid begged, tears already gathering in those big, brown eyes. "Tell him it's not true about my mother, Sarah."

"I wish more than anything that I could, honey, but I don't know what happened that day," Sarah answered honestly. "All I know is that your father loves you, Rashid."

"Isn't that sweet?" Nashemia caught Rashid's chin in her hand. "Your mother made a deal with the Al Asheera. If they would help her kill your father, she would rule the country with her son at her side. And make sure both she and the Al Asheera grew rich in the process."

"That's a lie!" Rashid screamed. "I don't believe you!" He tugged at his bound hands, trying to break free.

"Unfortunately, for Saree, your nanny managed to get you safely out of the palace with your Aunt Anna. Your father refused to give up your whereabouts, so your mother had him tortured. When that didn't work, she had a woman put in the cell next to his. Your uncle Hassan told Jarek that the woman was your mother. All night long, your father listened to the woman scream as they tortured her."

"It took her ten hours to die," Oruk added with a smugness that brought bile to the back of Sarah's throat.

"Of course, at the time, Jarek had no idea the extent of Saree's betrayal." Murad stood up and poured himself another glass of wine. "He didn't find out until he escaped from his cell and found her in his office holding you. Perfectly healthy. No marks or abrasions on her face."

"You're all lying," Rashid argued, but the sobs were coming full force and Sarah knew he believed them. "She would not. She was killed by the Al Asheera—"

"She was the leader of the Al Asheera. Her and your uncle Hassan. And your father's cousin, Zahid."

"Your father killed her," Murad repeated. "She begged him not to shoot her, but he smiled and pulled the trigger anyway."

"That's not true!" Rashid screamed and jerked on Sarah's arm, trying to free himself. "My father is king of Taer! He is royal. We protect our people."

"Your father can't even protect you." Nashemia laughed. "Your father is a murderer. Nothing more, nothing less."

"SARAH," Rashid whispered, his breath coming in short gasps between hiccups.

Five minutes had passed since Nashemia, Murad and Oruk had left them to prepare for their arrival at the drill site.

"Yes, honey?"

"What Nashemia said about Papa, it isn't true."

"Parts are not true, Rashid. Your father is not a murderer."

"He will save us, right?"

"Yes, but we should try and save ourselves, so they can't make a trap for him."

"How?"

"I don't know yet, but I'm working on it, kiddo."

"I have to tell you something."

"What?"

"I took your jade necklace. I wanted you to stay and knew that it was special to you. I figured you wouldn't want to leave something you loved so much. And if you stayed long enough, you and Papa would fall in love. Then we would be a family."

"Oh, Rashid. Love doesn't work that way." Sarah leaned

her cheek against the top of his head and closed her eyes against the tears. "Even if your father and I never get along, I will love you forever. And I will always be a part of your life, if you let me."

"Promise?"

"I promise." She rubbed her cheek against his hair. "When this is over we'll figure out a way to spend time together."

"What are we going to do about my papa, Sarah?" He scooted around until he could see her face. "I'm scared he will die."

"He won't," she reassured him, hugging him close. "We'll figure out a way to help him. But whatever we decide, promise me you will do as I say from here on out."

"I promise."

The rumbling of the train slowed, then came to a stop. Suddenly, a light flipped on in the compartment.

"Now isn't this touching?" Murad shook his head. "It looks to me like you have stolen the young prince's heart, too."

With a flick of a knife, he severed their bonds. "Let's go."

Once outside, Murad pushed Sarah and Rashid off the stairs of the train and onto the dirt.

Two of the Al Asheera reached down and dragged them to their feet. Sarah looked up and gasped at the laser-blue eyes that flicked over her.

"Come on," the man growled.

Al Asheera rebels were everywhere. Spread out in small groups throughout the drill site. Red scarves draped their faces, leaving only their eyes glinting, like rabid wolves, in the darkness.

In the middle lay Booker McKnight and about thirty of his men. Each on their stomachs, their hands bound by plastic zip ties behind their backs.

"Are they dead?" Rashid whispered to Sarah.

"Not yet," Murad answered for her. "But they will be. Just as soon as your father gets here."

Sarah slid her hand over her pockets, seemingly wiping them on the cotton. "Why do you need Jarek here?"

"News will break tomorrow that a group of men led by Booker McKnight took over the site, killed the workers and threatened the king."

Booker let out a stream of curses. One of the soldiers, a big man, yanked Booker up by his hands then slammed him back onto the ground. "Be quiet." The order was low and guttural.

Murad nodded at his soldier, pleased. "Booker McKnight is a suspected member of the Al Asheera. He and his men killed everyone. Including you, Miss Kwong, an innocent bystander who happened to be on a tour with the king and his son."

"They have him!" Oruk yelled the warning from the rear of the train.

"It's about damn time." Murad stood to the side as two rebels entered the circle and threw Jarek to the ground. Like Booker, his hands were bound behind his back with plastic ties at the wrists.

"Did he come with anyone?" Murad asked, his eyes searching the perimeter.

"No, he flew the plane in himself," one of the men answered. "Arrogant, isn't he?"

"He might be arrogant, but he's not stupid." Murad snorted. "He wouldn't come by himself. Quamar is around here somewhere. Tell your men to spread out over the area and find him."

"Quamar isn't here. He took his wife to the States." Jarek sat up. He spit blood into the sand.

"Jarek," Sarah whispered. Her eyes traveled over him, looking for injuries in the firelight but saw none.

"Are you both okay?"

When she nodded, he turned back to Murad. "You're wasting your time if you send men out there. I came by myself. I wouldn't risk the life of my son."

"You won't be offended if I don't believe you, Your Majesty." Oruk nodded to all but a few men. "Do as Murad says. Patrol the perimeter. I want Quamar found."

"Send them all, Oruk. We can keep these few covered. If Quamar isn't caught, our plans are destroyed."

Oruk nodded to the four remaining, including Blue Eyes. "Go on."

Reluctantly, they lifted their weapons and headed out.

Feeling his stare, Sarah stole a glance at Blue Eyes and nearly choked when he winked at her.

"The first man that comes back with his body will receive a huge reward," Murad added for good measure.

The guards grunted in satisfaction. One slapped another on the back.

"You'll have them bloodying each other for the prize now," Oruk observed, disgusted.

"Don't I know you?" Jarek's eyes narrowed on the Al Asheera leader.

"You've seen me before, under similar circumstance but we were never formally introduced, Your Majesty." Oruk bowed his head in a mock salute.

Suddenly, Jarek remembered. "You were the guard. The one that worked with Hassan and Saree. The one who tortured the woman in the cell next to mine."

"I am." Oruk lifted a negligent shoulder. "You could say I was learning the ropes from your uncle Hassan."

"You are behind this, then?"

"No, Your Majesty…" A woman stepped from the edge of the darkness, her smile cynical, her gun held level at Jarek. "That would be me."

"Nashemia," Jarek murmured. "Now I am surprised."

"It seems your life will always be cluttered with women who hate you," she smirked. "Including Miss Kwong."

"Is that why you framed her for the espionage? Using the tracking device, then later the recorder?"

"Oh, yes, the recorder." Nashemia crouched in front of Jarek. She ran the tip of the pistol down his nose, then over his lips, in a light caress. "I've never considered myself a voyeur before, but I have to admit I was disappointed when Trizal spoiled your little tête-à-tête with her."

She straightened and pointed the gun at Sarah. "Ramon put the tracking device in your purse just in case we weren't able to kill you both in the plane crash. Of course, I didn't know at the time Jarek dodged your meeting to take a ride out in the desert."

"If that's the case, why did Ramon avoid the rockets? Why did he try to save Sarah?" Jarek prodded. "Did he decide you weren't worth dying for?"

"Ouch, now that hurt, Your Majesty." But her mouth slid into a sly smile. "Maybe you're right. Once he got up in the air, he had a change of heart. Maybe he liked you, Sarah. Maybe he liked you more than me. Which would be surprising, actually."

"Not really," Sarah said sweetly. "I can't believe many people like you, Nashemia."

"You did. Until I gassed you." The other's woman smile tightened into a thin line. "Ramon was a simple man. All he wanted was for his daughter to live a better life than he and his brother had. I guess you could say that most fathers promise their daughters a kingdom. Mine gave me one."

Jarek froze. "Ramon was your father?"

"Oh, he was much more than that," Nashemia admitted. "He was your mother's lover, Jarek. Your mother had an affair with Ramon before she'd been promised in marriage to the new King of Taer. Bari had just abdicated, so Makrad needed to marry, soon, to ensure the royal line.

"I am your big sister, Jarek," Nashemia purred. "I have the DNA to prove it. Of course, I didn't find out until after Sandra Haddad diagnosed my father with cancer. I guess facing death makes people reevaluate their life, now doesn't it?"

"You are not royal, Nashemia." Jarek's laugh was little more than shards of glass against his vocal cords. "Not if you are my mother's daughter. My father held the royal bloodline."

"Who will protest my bid for the crown? You? My sweet little nephew, Rashid?" Nashemia tsked. "My legitimacy will not matter, considering those who have legitimate blood ties will be dead. With the exception maybe of Bari. But he is an old man now. I have few worries about his interference."

"And Bash?"

"Yes, Bash. Poor Bash," she mocked. "That was sad, was it not?"

"You killed him." Sarah made the statement.

"No, I liked him, actually. Oruk killed him," Nashemia corrected. "Or at least put him out of his misery. That bomb was a nasty business. It was meant for Jarek, of course. I actually went to see Bash, just so I could imagine the King of Taer lying there with half the skin burned off his body."

"That's why you were there that day?" Sarah stated. "But the tears—"

"Simple frustration," Nashemia answered and glanced at Jarek. "I never expected that you would be so hard to kill, brother."

"Bash just happened to be in the right place at the right time," Oruk inserted, coming up behind Nashemia. He curved a possessive arm around her waist. "I followed Sarah to the hospital that night." His eyes flickered to Sarah. "You have no idea how close you came to death, too. I would say a knife blade away."

"You can thank me for that, Miss Kwong. I called Oruk just before he was going to slice your throat," Nashemia countered. "I felt Roldo's death was a slight miscalculation on our part and your death would just bring more…attention. We decided we needed a diversion from the investigation. Nothing big, you understand. Just enough to give us another day or two."

"Oruk decided to use your lover as bait, Your Majesty," Murad added. "It was brilliant, actually."

"I never suspected Sarah of murdering Bash," Jarek commented.

"Oh, the bait wasn't for the murder," Nashemia corrected. "Servants talk. Even in a well-run palace such as your own. It was pretty obvious to your staff that you and Sarah were developing feelings for one another."

"That in itself gave us some additional leverage," Oruk inserted. "Love is always a distraction. Good or bad. I think you would have moved swifter with the investigation if Sarah hadn't been a distraction. We relied on your own prejudices from your experience with Saree to do the rest."

"Once burned, twice stupid," Nashemia joked.

"Of course, we had intended to kidnap the prince. But we couldn't find him in his bedroom. Lucky for us he decided to save your lady." When Nashemia went to ruffle

Rashid's hair, he jerked his head away. Angry, she grabbed a handful and held him in place. Rashid made no sound.

"Brave, aren't you?" She let go of his hair. "Be polite, little prince or I'll make your last few minutes with your dad very painful."

Nashemia waved her hand. "Kidnapping Miss Kwong served a duel purpose for us. With her ties to America and your being lovers—"

Sarah stiffened.

"Oh," Nashemia remarked with false surprise. "You didn't think anybody knew, did you?"

Murad stepped up. "All right. Enough of the conversation. We have very little time before sunrise to accomplish our plans."

"One more thing before we start." Oruk glanced at Nashemia, then leveled his pistol at Murad. "We've decided, three partners is one too many. Right, Nashemia?"

"Right, lover." Nashemia walked over to Oruk and briefly kissed him full on the mouth.

Suddenly, her gun exploded between them. Oruk dropped his pistol and stumbled back. "You bitch!" He grabbed for her, but lost his balance and went to one knee. Nashemia leveled the gun and fired again.

Oruk fell to the ground, his body unmoving.

"Remind me, darling," Murad commented, his tone bland. "Not to turn my back on you."

"No worries, Murad. He had the manpower, but you have the money." Nashemia stepped past Oruk. "Isn't it time?"

"Yes," Murad agreed. "The train is ready to take us back. Oruk must have been wrong about Quamar."

She turned the gun on Jarek, then glanced down at Oruk. "It's too bad you shot their leader, Jarek, before we could stop you."

"They won't be happy," Murad scoffed.

"I suppose you would like to die with your son and lover?"

Jarek said nothing.

Suddenly explosions hit the drilling grounds. One after another they ripped across the site in a semi circle of flash and fire. Some men screamed as their robes caught the flames, while others tumbled over the ridge surrounding the site.

"I think you have my answer," Jarek replied, his eyes pinning Murad with contempt.

"What is it?" Nashemia shrieked. "What's happening?"

Booker rose from the dirt, a knife in his hand. "Looks like an Al Asheera weenie roast to me."

Without warning, men crested the dunes, brandishing curved blades, wearing indigo scarves.

"Bari's men," Nashemia yelled as the swell of fighting soldiers swallowed her whole. "Stop them!"

Moments later, Quamar and Ian, then Cain and Jordan formed a circle surrounding Jarek, Sarah and Rashid. The four men fought back to back protecting those in the center.

"Ian," Jarek ordered, then raised his bound wrists. With a swipe of the sword, Ian severed the plastic.

Quamar tossed him a knife. Quickly, Jarek freed Sarah and Rashid's bindings.

"Get Rashid out of here." Jarek grabbed his son and pushed him toward Sarah. "Take him somewhere safe."

"But Papa—"

"Now!"

"Rashid." Sarah grabbed his arm. "We must do as your father says!"

Rashid stood, his fist tight at his sides. "I love you, Papa. Even if you had to kill my mama."

Jarek froze, his eyes found Sarah's. When she nodded, he grabbed Rashid and hugged him. "I love you, too. Don't ever forget that."

Jarek let his son go. "Stay with Sarah."

"Keep yourself safe, too," he warned as he pushed the boy toward Sarah. Jarek grasped her nape and pulled her close for a quick, hard kiss.

Booker yelled a warning. Sarah and Jarek turned just in time to see Booker shove a sword in the back of an Al Asheera soldier. As the man fell to the ground, Booker looked at Jarek. "We could use some help, Your Majesty."

"Booker?" Sarah shook her head confused. "How did you—"

"I work for Cain."

Chapter Eighteen

When they reached the train, Sarah started checking the crevices and windows to make sure no soldiers were hidden.

"Are we safe, Sarah?"

"For now—"

Pain exploded in Sarah's head. She stumbled back onto the ground.

"Not safe enough." Nashemia jumped from the steps of the passenger car. "Nothing like a quick kick to the head for a reality check."

"Run, Rashid." Sarah grasped a handful of sand and stood.

"No. I won't leave you, Sarah."

"Do as you're told," Sarah snapped. "Keep your promise."

Crying, Rashid nodded, then scrambled under the train.

"He won't get far," Nashemia promised. "Murad's out there somewhere."

"He's the least of your concerns," Sarah warned.

Nashemia reached in her boot and pulled out a long knife. She waved her fingers to Sarah. "Come and get me," she purred.

Sarah stepped in and let the sand fly from her hands.

Nashemia shrieked and grabbed for her eyes.

Sarah charged, knocking the knife from the other woman's hand and slammed her into the train.

"You bitch!" Nashemia screamed and backhanded Sarah. Pain exploded through Sarah's cheek, causing her to loosen her hold.

Nashemia gripped Sarah's throat and squeezed. "Now you die."

Choking, Sarah grasped Nashemia's wrists. Oxygen locked in her chest. Blindly, she reached out and snagged Nashemia's hair and yanked.

Nashemia cried out and grabbed her head as chunks of hair broke free in Sarah's fists.

Sarah stumbled back, dragging air back into her lungs.

"We're not done yet." Nashemia stood a few feet away. Blood oozed from a bald spot on her head, trickled down to her forehead.

Sarah dropped the hair from her hands. "That must have hurt."

The other woman wiped the blood from her face, looked at it on her hand. "Not as much as this will." Nashemia snagged the knife from the ground and raised her hand.

Suddenly, a gun exploded from behind Sarah. Nashemia screamed and fell back against the train. She dropped the knife and gripped her chest.

Sarah swung around in time to see Oruk fall to one knee. Blood covered his chest, dripped down his arms.

"Goodbye, lover." The gun dropped from his hand as he fell sideways in the sand. Dead.

Sarah ran over to Nashemia and kicked the knife away. It didn't matter, the woman lay propped against the train. She too was dead.

A scream ricocheted down the tracks. Sarah's blood chilled with realization. "Rashid!"

"Help me, Sarah!"

SARAH RACED DOWN THE TRACKS, her heart beating wildly when she saw Murad holding Rashid.

"At the risk of sounding cliché, I think here is where we get off." Murad placed his pistol against the little boy's temple and waved her forward with his free hand.

He then pulled ties from his pocket and threw them at her feet. "There is a bar up in the engine room. You're going to tie Rashid to it." Murad shoved the boy at her. "Now," he demanded. "Or watch him die from a bullet through his head."

Rashid hugged Sarah's waist, his body sobbing with fear. "It's all right, honey."

Sarah took his hand and led him up the stairs to a narrow corridor. The engineer lay dead on the floor.

"He had objection with me holding a gun on the boy, too," Murad commented. "Go!" He waved them down the narrow corridor to a steel pole at the front of the control panel.

"We're going to be okay, Rashid." Sarah placed the little boy's hands around the pole, then tied his wrists with the plastic.

"Now you."

Sarah placed hers by Rashid and Murad looped the zip tie around her wrists and pulled it tight.

"Now, just to make sure…" Murad yanked the plastic on Rashid's wrist, tightening them.

Rashid cried out and tugged on the bonds. Murad smiled and shoved the pistol into the waistband of his pants.

"Don't worry, if you're lucky you'll die in the explosion. And maybe not burn to death."

"You'll die, too," Sarah pointed out, tugging on her ties.

"I'll take my chances. I'm probably dead already," Murad reasoned, his tone bitter, his movements furious.

He disengaged the brake lever, then pushed the throttle up one notch. "Do you think Jarek and his friends won't hunt me down?"

Slowly the train picked up speed. Murad pushed the throttle forward three more notches.

Rashid glanced past her shoulder. "Sarah?"

"Don't worry, sweetheart." But Sarah caught the apprehension in the young boy's eyes. Instantly, she knew Jarek was at the end of the corridor.

She forced herself not to look. "If Jarek doesn't come after you, Jon Mercer will."

"Oh, I'm not worried." Murad slammed the throttle all the way forward and smiled when the engine picked up speed. He locked the throttle in place, then took conductor's keys from the control panel.

"Looks like we're all set." Murad dropped the keys in his vest pocket.

The train jolted, sending Rashid and Sarah crashing back. Murad looked up and swore. He grabbed his gun and aimed it down the corridor.

"Jarek!" Sarah tried to gain her balance as Murad fired six rounds. She glanced up, sighing in relief.

Jarek grabbed the engineer for protection, using the dead man as a shield.

Sarah kicked out at Murad, catching his arm and knocking the gun down under the control panel. "You bitch!" He slapped her across the cheek.

He slid open a side emergency door that led to a small ledge. "This is where I get off."

"The hell you do." Unable to fire his gun and risk shooting his son or Sarah, Jarek charged down the corridor. He threw himself at Murad and both of the men bounced off the wall of the engine compartment. Murad kicked out at Jarek, then scrambled out of the door.

Jarek went to the control panel and tried to bring the throttle back.

"He's got the key in his vest pocket," Sarah told Jarek. "You need to get it or the train will hit the dead end."

"I'll get it." Jarek took out his pistol and followed Murad up onto the roof of the train.

"Come and get me, Your Majesty," Murad yelled. Then, while Jarek watched, he jumped from the engine car to the first passenger car.

Jarek followed him, unable to fire his pistol. If Murad fell off the train, he'd take the key with him.

"Murad!" Jarek ran across the cars, jumping against the movement of the train.

The other man paused between the last passenger car and the first oil tanker. He glanced up the tracks. "You've got about three miles before we hit the barrier. I think we should just wait it out, Your Majesty." Murad patted his vest pocket. "Or would you rather wrestle for these?"

The train heaved, taking a curve too hard. Murad stumbled, tried to catch his balance, then screamed as he slid over to the side.

Jarek threw himself to the edge and caught Murad's wrist, but the man's momentum took him halfway over the side also.

"Give me the key!" Jarek struggled for leverage against the weight of the other man.

Laughing, Murad fought him, swinging wildly by one arm. "Let me go and I'll think about it."

"Not yet." Suddenly, Jarek released his grip with one hand and grabbed Murad by his tie. Murad struggled as the material tightened on his throat, fighting Jarek's grip with his free hand.

Jarek yanked harder, watching as Murad slowly strangled, gasping for his last breath.

Jarek pulled the body halfway up onto the car roof. He reached into the pocket and grabbed the key.

Without a thought, he let go and shoved the key in his pants pocket. Murad's body fell over the side, but Jarek didn't see. For the first time in a long time, he ran toward Sarah and Rashid. This time, Jarek hoped to save all three of them.

Chapter Nineteen

Sarah met the men in front of the palace.

"Are you ready?"

"Yes," she said, smiling at Cain. "Although I really don't need a three-man escort back to the States, Cain."

"It's all part of the package, ma'am," Ian quipped as he tossed her small luggage bag into the back of the black SUV. "Besides, you have a tendency to get in trouble when we aren't looking and I promised Lara I'd bring you back safe."

Sarah couldn't argue with the trouble part. It had been little more than twenty-four hours since Jarek had saved Rashid and her from the train.

She found out later that Quamar had sent word to Bari once they'd discovered she'd been kidnapped. Then Quamar, Ian, Cain and Jordan overtook some of the Al Asheera at the airstrip and killed them. Then they'd dressed in the dead men's robes and infiltrated the drilling site.

Quamar and Jordan brought in Jarek, while Ian—or Blue Eyes, as she'd dubbed him at the site—and Jordan stayed with her and Rashid.

"Do I have time to say my goodbyes?" Tears threatened

to fill her eyes, so she slipped the sunglasses from on top of her head onto her nose.

"Absolutely," Cain answered and gave her a quick hug. "We'll leave when you are ready."

"I'll only be a moment, I promise." Any longer and Sarah knew she'd fall apart. And that is the last thing she wanted to do.

Quamar, Booker and Rashid waited for her near the drive.

"Where is Jarek?" she asked quietly.

"Gone." Jordan answered the question. "Never would have believed he was the type to cut and run."

"He isn't," Quamar noted as she approached. "Jarek felt it better to make the goodbye less…eventful, Sarah."

She nodded, but the hurt stabbed just under her heart. Yesterday, after they had returned from the drilling site, Jarek arranged for a contingent of guards to escort her and Rashid back to the palace. She hadn't seen Jarek since.

"I decided to leave most of the clothes for Anna, Quamar. Thank her for me when she gets back."

Quamar looked at her knowingly. "You would not accept them because Jarek gave them as a gift."

"Yes."

Quamar grabbed her into his big arms. "You will have to come back soon."

One of the hardest things she had to do was step out of the giant's arms. But she managed it. Barely. "The next time you are in Nevada, come visit." She set her shoulders, forced a smile on her face. They both knew she was never going to come back to Taer.

"We will. Anna doesn't like anyone knowing, but she is addicted to blackjack."

Sarah laughed, then turned to her guard, who had never

been more than a few steps away. "I think Bash would be proud of you, Ivan." She rose up on her toes and gave the young man a kiss. "One of these days you'll have to tell me how you managed sleep while you were protecting me."

"When I let Nashemia drug me." He shook his head in disgust. "I got plenty of sleep."

"But you've learned," she teased, then sobered a little. "And so have I, I think." She gave him a quick hug. "I am counting on you to protect your king. And your prince. And yourself. Got me?"

"Yes, mistress." He leaned over and gave her a kiss on both cheeks. "If you ever decided to come back, I will protect you, too. I promise."

"I'd like that." She stepped away from Ivan and walked to Booker. "So you're staying behind?"

"Yep, I decided I needed a vacation," Booker quipped. "Cain approved it just about the time I was saving him from a knife in the gut."

"I think I owe you an apology, Booker."

"Why? Because for a while there, you thought I was a bad guy?"

"Yes," she said, smiling.

"Don't fool yourself, I am sometimes," he answered, but his grin was just a little too sharp with the truth. "But it's what I do best."

"Thank you for saving my life." Sarah glanced around at the men surrounding her. "All of you."

The men shifted their bodies just enough to tell her they were uncomfortable with the attention.

"It's what we do." Ian shrugged, breaking the moment.

"Sarah?" Rashid whispered. "Are you going to say goodbye to me, too?"

She squatted in front of the young boy. "I saved our

goodbye for last because I have something very special for you." Slowly, she unclasped the chain from her neck. "I want you to keep my jade necklace for good luck."

"Really?" Rashid had given her necklace back the night before, when they'd snuggled together in her bed. The last time, he promised, he'd use the laundry vent.

Sarah smiled at the memory and placed the stone in his palm. Then she covered it with her own.

"Really," she promised, her throat dry, her words hoarse from unshed tears.

Then he hugged her tight. "I love you, Sarah."

Sarah grabbed him close, knowing the tears she tried to check were trickling down her cheeks. "I love you, too, sport."

She pulled back and brushed a small cowlick from his forehead. Gently, she placed a kiss there. "Anytime..." She fought the emotion back, worked the words past the spasm in her throat. "Anytime you need me. Okay?" she whispered, unable to keep the thread of despair from weaving through her goodbye.

"Yes," Rashid agreed. With a grin, he glanced up at his uncle Quamar. "Soon."

JAREK PLACED his arm against the side of the office window sill and leaned forward. From his position, he watched Sarah say her goodbyes, quietly drinking in her features from a distance.

She wore stone-gray, wide-legged trousers, with a sheer lace wraparound blouse that tied at the waist, accenting her slim hips, the graceful line of her arms and back.

Her hair was down, hanging in a long, black sheet of silk over one shoulder.

The hug between her and Rashid hit him in the gut. He fisted his hands to keep himself from going outside.

"They are leaving, Your Majesty," Trizal said quietly from behind him.

"Is everything ready?"

"Yes, Prince Rashid and Master Quamar said they would wait for you down at the helicopter pad."

Jarek nodded.

"Miss Kwong left this for you, Your Majesty." Trizal walked over and handed Sarah's recorder to Jarek.

"Thank you, Trizal." Jarek gripped the device in his hand. "I'll be ready in a moment."

"Yes, sir."

After the door closed, Jarek pushed the play button. Nashemia's voice filtered through the room.

A small smile tugged at the corner of his mouth. Sarah had recorded the conversation at the drilling site.

Without hesitation, he hit the delete button on the recorder. No matter the outcome, the nightmares of Saree's betrayal were finally gone.

Sarah had taken care of that.

Chapter Twenty

Jarek ordered his airplanes and helicopters grounded. The drive to Morocco was going to be a long one.

But Quamar had insisted Jarek's soldiers had cleared all the rebels from the hills. Leaving the road safe to travel.

In all honesty, Sarah hadn't minded the idea of the drive. She'd grown to love the desert and wanted to see just a little more before she left for good.

"You all right?" Ian asked the question. He sat next to her in the backseat, while Cain drove and Jordan rode up front in the passenger seat.

"Yes. Thank you all again."

Ian took her hand in his and squeezed. "You know that Lara and I consider you family, right?"

"Yes," she said, swallowing against the unbending muscles in her throat.

"And family is always honest with each other."

"Yes."

"Then I have to tell you something."

"What?"

Ian sighed, a hint of sympathy in his blue eyes. "You're being stupid."

Sarah stiffened, then tugged her hand away.

"I have to agree with Ian, Sarah," Jordan inserted from the front seat. "It's obvious you love Jarek and Rashid. Why not fight for them?"

"I have my reasons." She looked out the window, watched the land speed by in a flat blur of beiges and browns.

"What reasons?"

"Are you talking about how Saree betrayed Jarek five years ago?" Ian asked.

She looked at the men one at a time. "You know. All of you know?"

"Booker told us in his debriefing that Nashemia took pleasure at filling you in," Cain admitted, his eyes on her through the rear view mirror.

"Please don't tell anyone." Fear tripped, then slid through her. "It would shatter Jarek and Rashid."

Ian hugged her to his side. "Relax, honey. We were there when it happened. We're certainly not going to start telling tales now."

"You were there?" She studied the men in disbelief. "All of you were there?"

They nodded in unison.

"Quamar managed to escape with Anna and Rashid, but before they did, he sent word to us through Sandra Haddad. We flew out to Taer immediately."

"Does President Mercer know?"

"Yes, he knows."

Anger started flickering through her limbs, then surged up her spine. "He knew before he sent me out to meet with Jarek?"

Cain sighed. "Yes, he's known for five years."

"Was this some kind of test?" Sarah demanded. "To see how ethical I could be? Did he think I wouldn't uncover the big secret in Jarek's past?"

"We all knew you would uncover it," Cain reasoned. "Most reporters worth their salt would, after spending time with Jarek and Rashid. Jon Mercer was just betting that you wouldn't use it as a stepping-stone in your career, like most might."

"You were protecting Jarek," Sarah realized.

"No, we were banking on the fact you would," Cain explained. "Just like you protected Lara after the biochemical scare a few years ago."

"He's family," Ian added.

"I'll be damned." Jordan laughed and nodded toward the front of the car. "It looks like your family just expanded."

Cain swore and hit the brakes, then slammed the gears into park. "I think Jarek has a problem with your leaving, Sarah."

"No he doesn't, he didn't even say goodbye—" She stopped when the men opened their car doors. "What are you talking about?"

"See for yourself."

Sarah unbuckled, opened the door and stepped out.

A hundred men lined the desert, blocking their route with a huge semi circle. All on camels or horses. All carrying swords, drawn and raised.

In the middle was Jarek on Taaj. On his right, sat Rashid. His left, Bari and Quamar.

"Oh, my God," Sarah murmured. "What is he doing?"

Jarek raised his hand and in one movement the soldiers moved forward on their animals.

Ian hugged her to his side. "I think that's his way of saying he loves you."

"Sarah! Sarah!" Rashid waved to her from the back of Ping's back. "Guess what? We're kidnapping you."

"You're what?" She squeaked the question.

"We're taking you captive, like Grandpa Bari did in the old days."

"Not so old, young man," Bari exclaimed, indignant.

"Who are all of those men?" Sarah whispered.

Cain grunted. "More than half are the palace guards, the rest are Bari's people."

"Still won't make up for the fact he arrested her," Jordan mused. "Poor bastard."

"I wouldn't be so sure," Ian murmured, sharing a deep pity for what Jarek was about to go through. After all, they had all been in Jarek's shoes at one point over the past few years. "This is going to be one hell of an apology."

Slowly, Jarek nudged Taaj forward. His scarf hung loose against one shoulder.

He stopped less than ten feet away. His coal-black eyes eagle-sharp and intense. "So are you going to come peacefully, or am I going to have to use force?"

Not able to stop herself, she took a step back. "Are you out of your mind?"

"Well, now there's a question." Jarek leaned one forearm over the pummel of his saddle. "One I've asked myself for the past five years," Jarek admitted.

"The few days I spent in that cell being tortured, I came about as close to insanity I imagine as any man could. But I made it through with the help of friends…" he nodded toward the men behind her "…and family." He tilted his back toward Bari, Quamar and his son. "I came out with scars, but I came out sane."

"Jarek." She closed her eyes, hoping she was just having a bad dream. "You can't kidnap me. It's just not done."

"Kidnapping is a harsh word. Let's just say I'm taking you somewhere quiet, somewhere the two of us can have a private conversation."

"And if I say no?"

"Then we have that same conversation right here." With a wave of his hand, one of his soldiers came forward with a video camera. He pointed it at Jarek.

"What are you doing?"

"Giving you an exclusive interview in which I will answer any question you have for me. Honestly. Without evasion."

"I'm done asking questions." Sarah frowned. "And you can't force me to do an interview."

"Not just any interview," Jarek countered, with more than a little arrogance. "I have no doubt after all the reporters I've denied, your interview will shoot you to the top in your field."

"Is that why you're doing this? You still believe this has been about my job?" That hurt more than anything.

"No. I'm fulfilling an obligation to you and Jon Mercer," Jarek argued. "If you do not conduct the interview, someone else will eventually. If I must do this, than I would rather do it with you. Someone I trust with my son's and my own life. This interview will affect Rashid just as much as me. But I realized keeping everything from him made him vulnerable. And it almost cost his life and yours."

"I gave you the recorder, so you must realize I have no intention of writing that story." Longing tugged at her belly, on its heels, a self-deprecating fury. "You went through all this trouble for nothing."

"I don't quite think you understand, sweetheart. I'm trying to clear up any misunderstandings or unfinished business before I ask you to marry me."

This time it was Sarah's turn to be surprised. "You said yourself, it's…us…," she stammered. "You and me…is impossible."

Jarek glanced at Ian. "She's cute when she stutters, isn't she?"

Ian laughed. "Flattery is not going to help her forget you arrested her, Jarek."

Jarek glared at his friend. "Shut up, Ian."

"This is impossible." Sarah shoved a hand through her hair in frustration.

"Not impossible. Just complicated." Jarek used her own words against her. "If the heir to the throne in England can marry a divorced woman, I certainly can marry an American. Times are changing for my country. And I have Bari and Quamar's support. They are respected, royal family members."

"You have to have more than acceptance to make a marriage work."

Jarek frowned when his three friends behind her nodded their agreement.

"She's right, Jarek."

"Stay out of it, Ian."

"I don't think I can," Ian said, his tone amiable, his stance anything but. "Since Sarah has no family present, we're prepared to play that role." He nodded at the men on either side of him.

Sarah looked back to see Ian, Cain and Jordan step up behind her, all three of them with their arms folded. All three faces set into hard lines.

She groaned. "This is not real. This can't be happening." She swung back to Jarek. "Let me go home. Please. I don't want to interview you. I don't want to marry you."

"Fair enough. You won't have to ask one question." He glared at the three men behind her, daring them to say something. "After, you can leave."

"Promise her, Papa!"

Jordan snorted with laughter. Cain coughed.

"I promise, Sarah," Jarek said, his tone dipping into that husky timber that set her heart racing. "All my life I was groomed to be king. I never took a step without once considering how it would affect the people of my country first, then my family and lastly myself. Then I met you in New York. I didn't know what hit me. But before I could figure it out Hassan uncovered information about your job."

"He set you both up, Sarah," Quamar interrupted. "Hassan had already made arrangements for Jarek to meet Saree in college. You got in the way."

"I went after Saree with a vengeance," Jarek continued. "Partly because I was rebounding from our affair. And partly, I think, because she was different from you. Colder and maybe, because of that, safer. At the time I had no idea she had planned the whole relationship. Quamar found out recently, that Hassan had paid for Saree's education at Oxford just so she could meet me."

"She loved you?"

"No, she loved money. And the power. She just didn't like to share it."

"Like Nashemia."

"Worse," Jarek explained. "Marrying Saree was one decision I made for myself without taking anyone or anything else into account. The one thing I based on pure emotion."

"Love."

"No. What I felt for Saree was never that deep or that pure. I understand that now," Jarek answered. "I also understand a few other things."

"What, for instance?"

"After the rebellion." Jarek paused, then corrected himself. "After her death, I vowed never to make a decision without taking my country into consideration."

"What happened was certainly tragic, Jarek. But it was not your fault. You were left no choice," Sarah reasoned. "Nashemia told me and Rashid the story."

"Rashid and I had a long talk this morning about it. I think with time and love, he will grow to understand," Jarek added. "He also confessed to his penchant for using the laundry vents to eavesdrop." Jarek shook his head. "He told me he promised you he would not sneak around anymore. Is that true?"

"Yes, but he promised under duress while we were on the train. And at the time, he'd just found out about Saree."

"Did Nashemia tell you Saree killed my parents?"

"No." The very thought made Sarah sick to her stomach.

"Saree arranged for their accident after she found out she was pregnant with a son. She used me and would have used Rashid. Maybe eventually even harmed him, too."

"And now?" she asked, her tone flat. "Asking me to marry you isn't taking your country into consideration, Jarek. I'm a reporter."

"Yes, but I know your heart isn't in it anymore. It isn't who you are," Jarek insisted when she shook her head in disbelief. "You should consider changing occupations. Taer needs a queen."

"And what do you need?"

"To be loved."

"I don't think I can."

"All right. I understand." He swung down from Taaj and took the camera from his soldier. "Here. It is yours."

Sarah stared at the camera he held out to her. She had everything she ever worked for. The big scoop. The big secret exposed.

And still, she had nothing. Just a cold hard lump of nothing in the pit of her stomach.

"The drilling site is less than an hour away. I have a plane waiting there for all of you. It will take you wherever you want to go." Once again he offered the video camera.

This time Sarah took the camera from his outstretched hand and then turned away.

"For most of my life, I've kept to myself. How I felt, what I thought," Jarek yelled after her, his voice hoarse with desperation. "Now with my family standing behind me, and three of my closest friends standing in front of me, I need you to listen one last time to me, Sarah."

She stopped, unable to take another step. A sob welled up in her chest but she refused to let it free.

"And I'm going to say this in front of all of them. I love you, Sarah Kwong. And I haven't said that to anyone, except my son, in a very long time. And I will not say it to another woman as long as I live. I walked away from us eight years ago in New York because I was afraid. You're more courageous than anyone I've ever known, Sarah. Don't leave us."

She did not turn around, couldn't. She was scarcely able to breath through the band of fear that constricted her chest. Instead, she studied the horizon, saw the orange hues of the sunset.

She loved the desert. She loved Rashid and she loved Jarek. And never again would she ever say that to anyone, if she walked away now.

Slowly, the band in her chest eased, allowing her to take a deep breath.

While no one spoke, she felt every pair of eyes on her.

Slowly, she turned back. Jarek hadn't moved. She smiled through her tears. Even in humbling himself, he stayed arrogant like only a desert king could.

"May Allah keep you safe on your journey home, Sarah," he whispered in a low raspy voice.

"I think for the first time I am home, Your Majesty." Uncaring, she let the camera drop to the ground. "If you can handle complicated."

An instant later, Jarek gathered her into his arms. "I wouldn't have it any other way." He held her up and twirled her around.

Slowly, she slid to the ground. "I love you, Jarek."

"Yippee!" Rashid jumped off of Ping and rushed forward. He threw himself at his father and Sarah.

The soldiers behind them broke out into cheers.

"Are we a family now, Papa?"

"Yes, we're a family."

"Will you be my mama, Sarah?"

Tears blurred, then slid down her cheeks. Gently, Jarek kissed them away.

"I'd like that more than anything." Sarah threw her arms around both of them, her breath hitching with pure joy.

"What do you think of that, son?" Jarek hugged Rashid to him, enjoying both Sarah and his son in his arms.

Rashid glanced up at his father, then back at the army of men lined up behind them. The little boy grinned, his dimples flashing in the sunlight. "I think that destiny has many helping hands."

* * * * *

*Celebrate 60 years of pure
reading pleasure with Harlequin!*

To commemorate the event, Harlequin Intrigue® is
thrilled to invite you to the wedding of The Colby
Agency's J. T. Baxley and his bride, Eve Mattson.

That is, of course, if J.T. can find the woman who left
him at the altar. Considering he's a private investigator
for one of the top agencies in the country—the best of
the best—that shouldn't be a problem. The real setback
is that his bride isn't who she appears to be…and her
mysterious past has put them both in danger.

*Enjoy an exclusive glimpse of
Debra Webb's latest addition to*
THE COLBY AGENCY: ELITE
RECONNAISSANCE DIVISION

THE BRIDE'S SECRETS

Available August 2009 from Harlequin Intrigue®.

The dark figures on the dock were still firing. The bullets cutting through the surface of the water without the warning boom of shots told Eve they were using silencers.

That was to her benefit. Silencers decreased the accuracy of every shot and lessened the range.

She grabbed for the rocks. Scrambled through the darkness. Bumped her knee on a boulder. Cursed.

Burrowing into the waist-deep grass, she kept low and crawled forward. Faster. Pushed harder. Needed as much distance as possible.

Shots pinged on the rocks.

J.T. scrambled alongside her.

He was breathing hard.

They had to stay close to the ground until they reached the next row of warehouses. Even though she was relatively certain they were out of range at this point, she wasn't taking any risks. And she wasn't slowing down.

J.T. had to keep up.

The splat of a bullet hitting the ground next to Eve had her rolling left. Maybe they weren't completely out of range.

She bumped J.T. He grunted.

His injured arm. Dammit. She could apologize later.

Half a dozen more yards.

Almost in the clear.

As she reached the cover of the alley between the first two warehouses she tensed.

Silence.

No pings or splats.

She glanced back at the dock. Deserted.

Time to run.

Her car was parked another block down.

Pushing to her feet, she sprinted forward. The wet bag dragged at her shoulder. She ignored it.

By the time she reached the lot where her car was parked, she had dug the keys from her pocket and hit the fob. Six seconds later she was behind the wheel. She hit the ignition as J.T. collapsed into the passenger seat. Tires squealed as she spun out of the slot.

"What the hell did you do to me?"

From the corner of her eye she watched him shake his head in an attempt to clear it.

He would be pissed when she told him about the tranquilizer.

She'd needed him cooperative until she formulated a plan. A drug-induced state of unconsciousness had been the fastest and most efficient method to ensure his continued solidarity.

"I can't really talk right now." Eve weaved into the right lane as the street widened to four lanes. What she needed was traffic. It was Saturday night—shouldn't be that difficult to find as soon as they were out of the old warehouse district.

A glance in the rearview mirror warned that their unwanted company had caught up.

Sensing her tension, J.T. turned to peer over his left shoulder.

"I hope you have a plan B."

She shot him a look. "There's always plan G." Then she pulled the Glock out of her waistband.

Cutting the steering wheel left, she slid between two vehicles. Another veer to the right and she'd put several cars between hers and the enemy.

She was betting they wouldn't pull out the firepower in the open like this, but a girl could never be too sure when it came to an unknown enemy.

Deep blending was the way to go.

Two traffic lights ahead the marquis of a movie theater provided exactly the opportunity she was looking for.

The digital numbers on the dash indicated it was just past midnight. Perfect timing. The late movie would be purging its audience into the crowd of teenagers who liked hanging out in the parking lot.

She took a hard right onto the property that sported a twelve-screen theater, numerous fast-food hot spots and a chain superstore. Speeding across the lot, she selected a lane of parking slots. Pulling in as close to the theater entrance as possible, she shut off the engine and reached for her door.

"Let's go."

Thankfully he didn't argue.

Rounding the hood of her car, she shoved the Glock into her bag, then wrapped her arm around J.T.'s and merged into the crowd.

With her free hand she finger-combed her long hair. It was soaked, as were her clothes. The kids she bumped into noticed, gave her death-ray glares.

They just didn't know.

As she and J.T. moved in closer to the building, she

grabbed a baseball cap from an innocent bystander. The crowd made it easy. The kid who owned the cap had made it even easier by stuffing the cap bill-first into his waistband at the small of his back.

Pushing through the loitering crowd, she made her way to the side of the building next to the main entrance. She pushed J.T. against the wall and dropped her bag to the ground. Peeled off her tee and let it fall.

His gaze instantly zeroed in on her breasts, where the cami she wore had glued to her skin like an extra layer. A zing of desire shot through her veins.

Not the time.

With a flick of her wrist she twisted her hair up and clamped the cap atop the blonde mass.

"They're coming," J.T. muttered as he gazed at some point beyond her.

"Yeah, I know." She planted her palms against the wall on either side of him and leaned in. "Keep your eyes open. Let me know when they're inside."

Then she planted her lips on his.

* * * * *

Will J.T. and Eve be caught in the moment?
Or will Eve get the chance to reveal all of her secrets?
Find out in
THE BRIDE'S SECRETS
by Debra Webb
Available August 2009 from Harlequin Intrigue®

**We'll be spotlighting a different series every month
throughout 2009 to celebrate our 60th anniversary.**

LOOK FOR
HARLEQUIN INTRIGUE®
IN AUGUST!

To commemorate the event, Harlequin Intrigue® is thrilled
to invite you to the wedding of the Colby Agency's
J.T. Baxley and his bride, Eve Mattson.

Look for *Colby Agency: Elite Reconnaissance*

THE BRIDE'S SECRETS
BY DEBRA WEBB

Available August 2009

www.eHarlequin.com

HIBPA09

You're invited to join our Tell Harlequin Reader Panel!

By joining our new reader panel you will:

- Receive Harlequin® books—they are FREE and yours to keep with no obligation to purchase anything!
- Participate in fun online surveys
- Exchange opinions and ideas with women just like you
- Have a say in our new book ideas and help us publish the best in women's fiction

In addition, you will have a chance to win great prizes and receive special gifts! See Web site for details. Some conditions apply. Space is limited.

To join, visit us at
www.TellHarlequin.com.

REQUEST YOUR FREE BOOKS!

2 FREE NOVELS
PLUS 2
FREE GIFTS!

HARLEQUIN®

INTRIGUE®

Breathtaking Romantic Suspense

YES! Please send me 2 FREE Harlequin Intrigue® novels and my 2 FREE gifts (gifts are worth about $10). After receiving them, if I don't wish to receive any more books, I can return the shipping statement marked "cancel." If I don't cancel, I will receive 6 brand-new novels every month and be billed just $4.24 per book in the U.S. or $4.99 per book in Canada. That's a savings of close to 15% off the cover price! It's quite a bargain! Shipping and handling is just 50¢ per book.* I understand that accepting the 2 free books and gifts places me under no obligation to buy anything. I can always return a shipment and cancel at any time. Even if I never buy another book from Harlequin, the two free books and gifts are mine to keep forever.

182 HDN EYTR 382 HDN EYT3

Name	(PLEASE PRINT)	

Address		Apt. #

City	State/Prov.	Zip/Postal Code

Signature (if under 18, a parent or guardian must sign)

Mail to the **Harlequin Reader Service:**
IN U.S.A.: P.O. Box 1867, Buffalo, NY 14240-1867
IN CANADA: P.O. Box 609, Fort Erie, Ontario L2A 5X3

Not valid to current subscribers of Harlequin Intrigue books.

**Are you a current subscriber of Harlequin Intrigue books
and want to receive the larger-print edition?
Call 1-800-873-8635 today!**

* Terms and prices subject to change without notice. Prices do not include applicable taxes. Sales tax applicable in N.Y. Canadian residents will be charged applicable provincial taxes and GST. Offer not valid in Quebec. This offer is limited to one order per household. All orders subject to approval. Credit or debit balances in a customer's account(s) may be offset by any other outstanding balance owed by or to the customer. Please allow 4 to 6 weeks for delivery. Offer available while quantities last.

Your Privacy: Harlequin is committed to protecting your privacy. Our Privacy Policy is available online at www.eHarlequin.com or upon request from the Reader Service. From time to time we make our lists of customers available to reputable third parties who may have a product or service of interest to you. If you would prefer we not share your name and address, please check here. ☐

HI09R

 HARLEQUIN®

INTRIGUE

COMING NEXT MONTH

Available August 11, 2009

#1149 STEALING THUNDER by Patricia Rosemoor
The McKenna Legacy
Fearing his love is a curse, the charming cowboy avoids relationships—until he meets the one woman he can't live without. Now someone is threatening her life, and there is nothing he wouldn't do to protect her.

#1150 MORE THAN A MAN by Rebecca York
43 Light Street
His bride knows that her protective billionaire is no ordinary man, but she doesn't know all of his secrets. Can he trust her with the truth and shield her from his enemies?

#1151 THE BRIDE'S SECRETS by Debra Webb
Colby Agency: Elite Reconnaissance Division
A Colby Agency P.I. discovers that there is more to the woman he meant to marry than meets the eye, and he won't rest until he knows whether their relationship was a lie. But first he must find his runaway bride.

#1152 COWBOY TO THE CORE by Joanna Wayne
Special Ops Texas
He spent years serving his country in a special ops unit, but now this military man longs to return to his cowboy ways. Back home in Texas, his dreams of the quiet life are shattered when he meets a woman in danger…a woman who rouses all his protective instincts.

#1153 FAMILIAR SHOWDOWN by Caroline Burnes
Fear Familiar
Betrayed by her presumed dead—and double agent—fiancé, the ranch manager won't let another man lie to her. Now she learns that her new hire is really an undercover agent, and he's looking for the truth. Well, so is she! Will he be the last straw or her salvation?

#1154 NAVAJO COURAGE by Aimée Thurlo
Brotherhood of Warriors
To catch a serial killer, her department brings in a Navajo investigator. Although she may not agree with his methods, she can't ignore his unique skills or his sensuous touch. But the killer may be closer than they think….

www.eHarlequin.com

HICNMBPA0709